MR. OCTOBER

HEROES OF ROGUE VALLEY: CALENDAR
GUYS
BOOK 11

ANN ROTH

OLIVER-HEBER BOOKS

PUBLISHER'S NOTE: This is a work of fiction. Names, characters,
places, and incidents either are the product of the author's
imagination or are used fictitiously. Any resemblance to actual
persons, living or dead, business establishments, events, or locales is
entirely coincidental.

Mr. October Copyright 2025 © Ann Roth

Published by Oliver-Heber Books

0 9 8 7 6 5 4 3 2 1

Mr. October—Rob Carver
Age 34, 6'1", 192 pounds of muscle
Single
Proud Senior Firefighter
Time with Guff's Lake Fire Department: 15 years

Tuesday afternoon in mid-October, Jenny Carver's phone rang with a call that filled her with dread. Orchard High School again? "Hello," she said, schooling herself for whatever bad news the guidance counselor had for her this time.

"Hi, it's Debra Williams, Maddie's World History teacher. I met you and your husband at the open house in September."

Not the counselor, then. "I remember you. Hi. By the way, Rob is my *ex*-husband." Shortly before they'd graduated from the same high school, Jenny had discovered she was pregnant. They'd married right after graduation. "What can I do for you?"

"I'm calling for two reasons. First, Maddie wasn't in class today, and the office didn't receive a call. I hope she isn't sick."

"Not that I know of." Jenny was the one who felt

sick. No telling where her daughter had gone or what she might be up to. "Thanks for letting me know. I'll see what I can find out. What's the other reason?"

"Maddie's a smart girl, but she's not doing well in class. I don't want her to fail the course. We're having a big test next week that counts as thirty percent of her grade, and I've scheduled an after-school review of the subject matter for this Thursday. It's important that she shows up. I expect she mentioned this to you?"

Not a word. Maddie's freshman year had been no picnic, and the first six weeks of sophomore year seemed to be off to an even worse start. She was going to read that girl the riot act. Who said twins were alike? Fraternal twins, Maddie and Britt were as different as day and night. "I appreciate you letting me know. She'll be there."

As soon as the call ended, Jenny texted Britt, who'd just finished with her biweekly extreme Frisbee practice but wasn't home yet.

Your sister left school and missed World History. Any idea where she is?

The reply came immediately. *No, but she might be at Mr. Mister with Hudson and other friends.*

Hudson was Maddie's current boyfriend. Jenny had yet to meet him. The café wasn't far from the school and popular with kids for lunch and coffee. She didn't mind either of her daughters going there, but skipping class and failing to boot? Unacceptable.

She'd see Rob tomorrow morning, when he picked up Alcatraz, the collie he boarded with her during his weekly shift at Guff's Lake Fire Department, aka GLFD. Forty-eight hours on, the rest of the week off. Normally, she'd talk to him then, but she needed to update him now.

Within seconds, she contacted the firehouse. Miranda, the woman at the front desk, answered the phone. She also kept track of the people who came through the door for one reason or another as well as each firefighter's schedule.

"It's Jenny," she said when Miranda answered. "Is Rob available?"

"It's been a while. Nice to hear your voice. Perfect timing. He just woke up from—I'll let him tell you. Hang on."

Moments later, her ex-husband came on the line. "Hey," he said in the lovely deep voice she knew so well. They'd been divorced thirteen years and managed to be marginally civil to each other for their kids' sake. The therapy she'd had after her mother's death four years earlier had helped her learn how to manage her irritation without getting too upset with Rob, a co-parenting necessity.

Not that they always got along around the girls, but they tried. Over the years, they'd discovered that limiting their time together or talking on the phone, usually about the kids, worked best. Rob had them every other weekend, and the girls spent holidays going from one house to the other. The rest of the time, Jenny had them.

Handling the bulk of raising them hadn't been easy when they were little, and so far in their teen years had become even harder. In their eyes, she was the bad guy while Rob could do no wrong. Although he'd turned into a fairly decent father, she was still the one to bear the brunt of disciplining them when they needed it. "You sound tired."

"Rough night, but so far today, things are less hectic. I was able to sack out for a few hours. I'm still groggy from that. There was a house fire in the middle of the night. We managed to contain it and get the family out safely, but there's a significant amount of damage to the home."

"What a shame. Let's hope they qualify for help from the benefit fund." A number of the good people in Guff's Lake donated regularly, but the bulk of the funds came from the calendar that featured a different firefighter each month. This year's guys were from Rob's shift, which worked out well, as there were twelve teammates total. When the year ended, a different team would take their place. Rob was Mr. October. They were all hotties, and no woman in town could resist owning a copy—herself included. "I'm glad you managed a nap. It's a good thing your shift is almost over."

Her ex and five of his colleagues boarded their dogs with her during their shift. Guys from other teams did the same during theirs, weekends excluded. Jenny and Alicia, a friend and dog walker she employed, helped take care of the boarded dogs and the additional canines they picked up for weekday walks. Between the dog business, Fashion Dogs, the doggie outerwear company Jenny owned and managed, and Rob's child support, she was able to pay the bills and save some, too.

"I'll bet you didn't get outside much today," she added.

"Not really."

"I hope you'll get a chance to while it's still daylight. It's a gorgeous fall day, clear and not too cold yet, and the view of Guff's Lake and the Siskiyou Mountains is spectacular."

"I'll bet," Rob said. "This is a nice time of year to get out and hike around the lake."

The lake, which was also the town's namesake, was a huge tourist draw for the Oregon town of just under twenty thousand. "When Alicia and I walked the dogs this morning, we ended up staying outside longer than usual because we couldn't bear to go inside quite yet. Alcatraz has missed you."

"When he's with me, he misses you. I know you didn't call to chit-chat. What's up?"

"Debra Williams, Maddie's World History teacher —we met her on Parent-Teacher night—called to let me know Maddie wasn't in class today."

"That's not good."

"Oh, it gets worse. She's failing the class. There's a test next week that counts as a third of her grade. To help her students, Mrs. Williams has scheduled an important review of the material for after school Thursday. She expects Maddie to be there, and we—I mean I—need to make sure that happens."

"What's your plan?"

"Drive her there myself and wait to take her home. I don't trust her enough to drop her off and come back after the review. If your schedule allows and you want to come help ..." Rob owned a mobile car detailing business on the side and spent his days away from the station working and overseeing that. Between running her own two businesses and taking care of the girls, Jenny was pretty busy herself, but this was a big deal. "I could use your support."

"Sure. I might have to reschedule an appointment or maybe Daniel will fill in for me if he hasn't scheduled something of his own at the same time. Either way, I'll be there." After a brief pause, he added, "I'll pick you up, and we'll go together, a unified front. That way, waiting for Maddie to finish the review will be less boring."

Uncomfortable, too. Therapy only went so far. They got along pretty well, but hanging out with him wasn't something she enjoyed. She needed him, though, to back her up when Maddie had fits about getting dropped off and picked up. Not that she had another way of getting there and back. Carpooling for this wouldn't do. "Okay," she said.

"What're you planning to say to her when she gets home this afternoon?"

"I'm going to let her know I'm disappointed and ground her, of course, from everything except going to classes. No after-school yearbook meetings or art." Two activities Maddie enjoyed.

"Gonna ask her where she was?"

"You bet I am. I'll text you when I find out more."

"Do that," he said. "She needs to learn a lesson, but she's gonna flip."

Even the thought was unpleasant. "It won't be the first time. There are consequences to certain actions, and she needs to learn that. I'll see you Thursday."

WHEN ROB'S shift ended at seven a.m. Wednesday morning, he and Daniel headed to Rosemary's Breakfast Nook, which wasn't far from the firehouse. The Nook served the best breakfasts in town, and weather permitting, opened at six a.m. daily. Big supporters of the GLFD, the café posted the calendar prominently above the display case.

Breakfast the morning after the shift ended was always enjoyable, and like the rest of the crew, Rob attended when he could. That morning, he and Daniel were the only ones who made it. Rosemary, the forty-something owner of the place, greeted them with a welcome smile. "Only two of you today?"

The rest of the guys had plans and seemed eager

to get home to their wives or girlfriends. Rob and Daniel were both single, so no big deal for them. "Just us," he said.

She nodded, showed them a table for two, and brought them water and coffee. No menus needed, as they were familiar with most of the selections. Any specials were written on a chalk board. As soon as Rosemary turned in their order, she bustled off to another table.

As no one else was joining them, they decided to have a business meeting over breakfast. Nothing firehouse related. Last year, Daniel had become Rob's right-hand man at the mobile detailing business. He was smart, steady, and competent, and Rob counted himself lucky to have the guy on board.

Daniel had a sad past. A few years earlier, after the tragic loss of his wife and wanting a fresh start, he and his dog had transferred from a firehouse in Sacramento and joined GLFD. Rob got along great with him. Their dogs liked each other, too. "Did you catch up on sleep last night?" he asked Daniel. At six feet four and age thirty, the guy topped him by three inches and had to shift his legs around to fit under the table.

"Like a baby. You?"

"Pretty well." He'd worried about Maddie and wished he knew why she was sabotaging her sophomore year. She'd messed up freshman year, too, but hadn't failed any of her classes. According to a text from Jenny last night, she'd learned that their daughter had been at Mr. Mister's. Why she'd skipped class for the place where she ate lunch daily was a mystery. "FYI, I'm going with Jenny to the high school Thursday afternoon and won't be available to take any detailing jobs after lunch."

"Good to know. Jenny's great. She takes real good care of Toad. I'll be picking him up when I leave here."

"Same."

"What's going on at the high school? Maddie again?"

Rob nodded. "She's failing one of her classes and was a no-show there yesterday."

"That's not good."

His bud had no idea. Rob felt partly responsible for the failure of his and Jenny's short marriage and what had followed. Things had been great till the twins had arrived six months after the wedding. Some two years later, their relationship had gone south. As it'd turned out, he'd sucked as a husband and father, which no doubt had affected their daughters. He'd spent the last thirteen years, a few of them working with a therapist, trying to make up for his failures. As if he could.

Breakfast ended, and he and Daniel went their separate ways. Before heading to Jenny's to pick up Alcatraz. Despite the gloomy clouds overhead, the house he'd once called home looked cozy and welcoming—glimpses of colorful rugs and comfortable-looking furniture through the picture window.

The usual wave of nostalgia hit him. This was where he and Jenny had lived as a married couple. At first, they'd been so happy, so in love and having great sex. A level of passion he hadn't experienced since. Back then, the house had been owned by her parents and rented to them at a very reasonable cost. As it turned out, for a price: Jenny's mother had controlled her. After the divorce, they'd sold it to her at a lower-than-market price.

Since then, both he and his ex had managed to get college degrees, his through the extension program at the University of Washington that led to promotions and more pay, hers at the community college in business and communications, both of which helped her establish her businesses.

Picking his dog up was always a joyful reunion, and the nostalgia faded.

As always, Jenny looked beautiful—slender with slightly wavy shoulder-length, light brown hair parted on the side. She and Rob were the same age. She hadn't aged a bit except to get even lovelier, whereas he looked every bit of his almost thirty-four years. No heterosexual man with eyes could help being attracted to her, himself included. That didn't mean he wanted her. He didn't, but there were times ...

"See you tomorrow afternoon," he told her and took off.

2

Thursday morning, after spending half a day detailing the classy BMW he worked on twice a year, Rob was ready to get outside with Alcatraz. It was a beautiful autumn day, warmish which was normal for mid-October, with a mild wind hinting at the cold to come. After an invigorating run, the collie settled in for a nap while Rob had lunch. Several hours after school let out at Orchard High, he headed to Jenny's to pick her and Maddie up. He arrived right on time, geared up and ready to face his daughter, regardless of her mood. Which, being forced to go to a review class she was failing, was bound to be glum at best.

"How are my two girls?" he said, smiling.

Home from Ultimate Frisbee practice, Britt, five foot nine with short amber hair and her mother's blue eyes, returned the smile. Maddie, five foot seven with shoulder-length dishwater blonde hair and his brown eyes, scowled as if he'd insulted her. Definitely a bad mood.

"Do you have to come, Dad?" she whined. "It'll be boring. Besides, you and Mom don't like being together."

He nodded at Jenny to reply. "We really don't mind, do we, Rob?"

"Not at all."

Their daughter's snort of skepticism let them know she didn't think so.

Time to change the subject. "What are you going to do while the rest of us are gone?" he asked Britt.

"Take a shower, do my homework, then text my friends."

Maddie grabbed a notebook and her World History textbook. No iPads or phones—her teacher didn't want anyone getting distracted. She didn't say much on the drive to the school, but he did. "I want you to pay attention in class and ask questions if you're confused. You're smart as a whip, and if you apply yourself—"

"I know, Dad," she interrupted. "You don't have to repeat what Mom already said, like fifty times."

"Attitude, missy," Jenny warned.

They made the remainder of the drive in silence. When they pulled up at the school and Jenny opened the passenger door to exit the car, Maddie cringed. "Please, Mom, don't come in with me. I promise I'll go to Mrs. Williams' classroom."

Rob gave a slight nod for Jenny to trust her on that. To his surprise, she did. "All right. Your dad and I will be right here when you come out in roughly an hour, according to Mrs. Williams."

❧

As soon as Maddie disappeared inside the high school, Jenny turned to her ex. He was still as good-looking as the day she'd met him eighteen years ago. Tall, buff, and hot. Yes, she was still attracted to him, but that was as far as it went. "What are we going to do for the next hour or so? I don't want to leave, and I didn't bring my iPad. We need to do something to pass the time."

"We never had to ask ourselves that in high school." He smirked. Then, "It's almost dusk and decent weather. Why don't we take a walk on the campus? I haven't done that since high school."

"Why not?" Outdoor lights lit a visible path around the parking lot, the building, and the football and track fields.

"Amazing how being out here makes me think of the past," he said as they started off. "Back then, we were crazy in love. We couldn't keep our hands off each other."

The last thing Jenny wanted was a walk down memory lane. "Don't remind me." She'd changed so much since then and had had plenty of experience over the years. But the truth was, sex had never been as good as it'd been with Rob. Their life had been sweet until the babies had arrived and the arguments had started. By the time they'd decided to divorce, they'd stopped touching each other entirely.

"I liked being married at first," he said after a few moments, almost as if they were on the same wavelength.

"Me, too." Sleeping beside the man she couldn't get enough of, making love without guilt whenever the need arose. Which had been at least once a day, even when Rob came home exhausted from his forty-eight-hour shift. Make-up sex when they argued ... It'd all been wonderful. "But when I look back, what I see are two eighteen-year-old kids way too young for marriage who used sex as a cure-all instead of working on how to solve our problems."

"Your mom didn't help, either."

She had to agree. "Learning to handle our relationship better isn't the only reason therapy helped me so much. I understand now that as a very young bride and mom, I wasn't strong enough to disregard her overbearing ways instead of working to create a united front with you. But at the time and us saddled with twins, she was a lifesaver. Your mom was a big help, too."

"She worked full time and did what she could. She also stayed out of our business. Yours made it a lot harder for us to be a family and work out our problems. It was always her way or the highway, always her up in our business. We didn't have much chance to figure things out. Besides, we were both too exhausted to do more than plod through the days and nights. You had to deal with our newborn twins and I did everything I could to earn more money for us. Firefighting was rigorous enough, and taking a second job at the hardware store was insane."

"Those were such hard days," she agreed. "We needed every penny of what you earned."

"That and time alone with only the two of us around."

"If you'd let her and Dad help with the finances—"

His jaw tensed. "Give her even more to criticize about me? I had my pride. Regardless, she didn't like me."

He wasn't wrong. Jenny's mother had never made a secret of her dislike for him, for all the good it did. Back then, nothing could keep them apart. But after the birth of the twins, her mother's opinion of Rob had driven an ever-widening wedge between them. Jenny glanced at him. "Half the time, she didn't like me, either. She thought we were way too young to get married, and she was right." Out of habit, she started to reach for his hand, then hastily slid her fists into her coat pocket. "It's nippy out here. Should've brought gloves."

"I have mine, if you want to borrow them."

Sometimes he could be so sweet. She almost wanted to kiss him. Shocked at herself, she stuttered to a stop.

Stopping as well, he gave her a sideways look. "You okay?"

Besides being out of her mind nuts? Must be the moon. She nodded. "I'm fine. I don't need your gloves, but thanks for offering."

The walk continued. "With both Maddie and Britt having boyfriends, we should emphasize our mistakes in the hope they won't make the same ones."

"That's what I've been doing since they were in middle school," Jenny reminded him.

"So have I, but now that they're older, it can't hurt to talk about it again."

"And we will. I've told them countless times how difficult it was to raise them when we were babies ourselves and that they should think about college. Britt has always been oriented toward getting more education, and I assumed Maddie would feel the same. Of course, that was before they started high school. Maddie sure has changed. I wish I knew why. Is it our parenting skills? We aren't exactly friendly to each other."

Rob shrugged as they crossed the football field. "For divorced parents, we're doing all right."

She gaped at him. "Maddie's grades haven't been the best. She seems to have lost her way, and I don't know how to help her. It would be nice if you'd weigh in with ideas." For once. "I'd like to hear them."

He shot a wary look her way. "Sure about that?"

"What do you mean?"

"You usually wave off my suggestions."

"I do not." After thinking about that for a moment, she agreed. "You're right, I do. Unfortunately, the subject never came up in therapy. It's a bad habit I learned from my mother. I'm sorry about that and promise to seriously consider whatever you come up with."

"I'd appreciate it. I could have pointed it out a long time ago, but I never did. Wish I could think of something that'd help us with Maddie. I'm in the dark, too, but I remember how screwed up I was as a kid. That's how we learn. I didn't exactly ace my classes, either. My parents weren't the best role models and were always on my case, which you know." He shook his head. "Being an only child sucked, something we have in common. My parents' constant monitoring backfired, big-time. When they punished me, I defied them and snuck out. So did you, by lying to your parents a lot. You made yourself believable because you had to —you were scared of your mother. I expect Britt will get into trouble, too."

Jenny cringed at the prediction. "Missing classes and failing? Don't say that."

"It's gonna happen."

"Maybe it won't. In case you've forgotten, I didn't even consider sneaking around until we got together, and I only did it to see you," she said, and sighed. "What other choice did I have? My mother was on me all the time about you." She was quiet a moment, thinking about the woman and the cancer that had stolen her life four years earlier at the age of fifty-four. "Regardless, I still miss her."

"I know, and I'm awful sorry she passed so young. Cancer sucks." He didn't speak again for several minutes. "Here's a thought—maybe your new boyfriend is the reason Maddie's acting up so much."

She threw him a dirty look. "Where did that come from? Shawn isn't my boyfriend. The girls know that." Although after dating him since late August, Jenny had grown to like him enough to want to get more deeply involved. After thirteen years of singlehood, and almost thirty-four years old—just around the corner from forty!—she was tired of being alone and ready to settle down with a nice guy. Someone she had decent chemistry with and could talk to without getting into a shouting match. Why not Shawn? "We're dating, that's all."

"The girls never say much about him. Do they like him?"

Jenny made a so-so gesture with her hand. "They aren't exactly warm and friendly to him, but they're like that with every man I date. I don't think they want to share me. They do the same thing to you."

"At times."

She eyed Rob. "I gather you don't like Shawn." She hadn't cared much for the females Rob dated, either. Especially Nora, the woman he'd briefly moved in with some two years earlier. Why, she didn't know. Their social lives were separate and didn't affect each other.

Rob shrugged. "Beats me. I only met the guy once."

"And yet, you have a negative opinion of him. That's not fair." Bristling, she shared another hot topic of hers. "You don't make life with Maddie any easier for me. You may be a big, strong guy and a crackerjack firefighter, but when it comes to the girls, you're a pushover."

"This is why I keep my opinions to myself." he

said. "What does that have to do with Shawn? Or do you just get off on insulting me?"

"It's not an insult, it's an observation," she pointed out. Then realized what was happening—they were falling back into old patterns best avoided. "Darn it, we're both riled up. We need to stop."

"I agree, but I also need to defend myself. Your so-called observation is an unfair one based on nothing factual, and you know it. I'm here tonight and supporting you in every way. I'll tell you what I think is causing Maddie's recent behavior—hormones. Remember us at fifteen? We thought we knew a lot more than our parents."

Striving for a calm note, she managed a laugh. "Boy, were we wrong. At least neither of the girls seems hot and heavy with their boyfriends like we were with each other."

"That we know of."

"Come on, Rob. If they were as hot and heavy into their guys as we were, don't you think we'd know?"

"Maybe, maybe not. Whether or not they feel that way now, with their hormones running amok, it's gonna happen. They've been learning about sex for years now, and it's good that we've reinforced staying safe and using birth control. We don't want them making the same mistakes we did."

"They're aware of that and understand how to be careful. Until I know otherwise, I'm going to trust them."

"We don't have a choice, do we? No more squabbling tonight—let's get along for Maddie's sake." His watch buzzed. "It's time we got back to the car. She should be finished soon. For all we know, she's already done."

They were some distance from the parking lot. "I

don't want her waiting in the dark." Jenny said. "We'd better run."

She tried to keep up with Rob, but she'd never excelled at running. After a minute, he doubled back. "Hurry, Jenny!" He reached for her hand and urged her along.

The first time he'd touched her in ages. She wasn't going to think about that now, just held on.

3

Whe they reached the Subaru and Rob dropped Jenny's hand, Maddie was waiting for them. "Where were you?" she asked, sounding put out.

He glanced at Jenny, but she was catching her breath, and he answered. "We needed to fill the time, so we took a walk around the whole campus. After all these years, it was fun to see. Orchard keeps the grounds so nice."

Their daughter glanced from him to Jenny. "How come you're out of breath and your cheeks are so red, Mom?"

Rob hadn't noticed before. He did now.

"Are they?" Jenny touched her face. "Exertion. Credit your dad for that. Time got away from us. We didn't want you to have to wait, so we ran. I've never moved that fast in my life." She glanced at him with a not unfriendly expression. "You really put me through the paces."

Running had been surprisingly fun, and he grinned. "I sure did."

Maddie looked from one to the other, the corners

of her lips lifting in an almost smile. Rob was puzzled. What was that about?

"How was the class?" Jenny asked in the car, turning half around in the passenger seat to see their daughter. "Did you learn things?"

A shrug. "I guess."

"Do you think it'll help with the exam?"

"Probably."

"I can quiz you if you want."

"No, Mom."

Maddie sounded angry, as she often did with her mother. He didn't like that and neither did his ex, but teens were easily irritated.

When they arrived back at Jenny's, Britt was full of chatter. "You guys were gone longer than I thought you'd be," she said when she finished telling them about her homework and things her friends had texted.

"Your mom and I took a walk around campus and were late getting back to the car," Rob explained.

It happened again—the corners of Maddie's lips lifted a fraction. "Would it be okay if we stayed with you tonight, Dad? We'll run upstairs now and pack our clothes and stuff."

Fine with him, if Jenny agreed. He glanced at her. "Okay with you?"

"As long as you keep Maddie off all phones and internet unless she's doing homework."

Maddie gaped at her. "I can't use my phone?"

"Sorry, kiddo, you lost that privilege. If you promise not to skip class again and pass the test with a grade of C or higher, you'll get it back."

"Can I at least bring my iPad?"

"No."

No sign of curling lips now, just a surly look. "How am I supposed to study?"

"The way your dad and I did before internet was added to most schools. You open the book and read."

"That's not fair. Some stuff is online."

Jenny didn't appear to have heard that. "I don't want her to use your phone or Britt's." she said, glancing at Rob.

"Not on my watch, unless you want a worse punishment." Still smarting from Jenny's crack about him being a pushover, which he occasionally was but only when he chose to be, he made sure to look each daughter square in the eyes. He wanted them to know he was in full agreement with his ex. "Got that?" Both of them nodded, and he added, "No TV, either. After you do your homework, you'll have to entertain yourselves with something to read, playing a board game, or doing a puzzle."

"Why am I being punished?" Britt muttered, her mood suddenly as sour as her sister's. "I didn't do anything."

Maddie smirked, and her sister gave her a dirty look. "One more word, Maddie, and I swear I'll say something."

Whatever that meant. Girls and their secrets. Maddie's hostility faded into a sad face. "How do you expect us to play games without an iPad?"

"Yeah, Dad, how?" Britt seconded.

"I have plenty of board games, which you already know, and a deck or two of cards. Also several thousand-piece puzzles. Bring a book or magazine with you or try one of mine."

Maddie made a face. "You don't read the kinds of books we like."

Neither of them seemed excited about the evening

ahead. "Are you sure you want to stay over at my house tonight?" he asked. "You'll be there all weekend."

The girls exchanged a look and nodded.

Jenny gave in surprisingly quickly. "You may as well pack, then." As the twins disappeared up the stairs, she frowned and lowered her voice. "You grabbed my hand when we ran toward the car."

"Well, yeah. We needed to hustle, and you were falling behind." Reaching for her had been automatic, which had surprised him after thirteen-some years of divorce. He regretted it now, mainly because he'd actually liked holding on to her. Weird as that was. "If you objected, you could've let go."

"I would've, but as you said, we needed to move quickly." She looked worried. "I hope Maddie didn't notice."

"I doubt she did," he assured his ex.

"I don't know—she made that comment about my red face and gave us that snarky smile."

"And you told her why."

"Yes, but I still worry. I don't want her getting any ideas about us."

"How could she? We're not together and never will be." To do otherwise would be a hell he never wanted to repeat. "She knows that."

"As she should. Are you sure you're okay with having them an extra night on top of the weekend?" she asked in a low voice.

"It's fine with me."

Thirty minutes later, after the girls loaded their stuff in the trunk, he was on the way home. Britt was in the front seat and Maddie in the back. They'd switch places next time.

"I'm curious," he said, glancing at them in the passenger seat and the rearview mirror. "Why do you want to come home with me tonight?"

"I'd rather be at your house—I need a break from Mom," Maddie said.

Rob understood but wasn't about to bad-mouth his ex, even though he disapproved of the way she harped on the girls nonstop when they messed up, after she'd already disciplined them. It reminded him an awful lot of her domineering mother. "She loves you both, and she's doing what she thinks is right." Too bad Jenny wasn't around to hear him defend her. "There are times when one or both of you need to be yelled at," he added, although not half as often as Jenny did it. He wished she'd lighten up some and let the consequences she handed out speak for themselves.

"Can we go out for pizza at Harvey's tonight? I'm super hungry," Maddie said.

"She was too nervous to eat today," Britt told him.

He was surprised. He'd never imagined that one of his teenage daughters might lose her appetite due to nerves. Poor kid. "Because of the review class tonight? What did you think would happen?"

"That Mrs. Williams would be mad at me for skipping Tuesday and talk about it to the other kids."

"Has she humiliated others in front of people before?" Maddie shook her head. "She'd never do it to you, either. I doubt she's mad. She's probably a little disappointed, though. Mostly, she knows how smart you are and wants you to do well, the same as your mom and I do." Maddie didn't react, and he added, "I know how awful it feels when you think you let someone down."

"How would you? You're a hero, with your photo in the Firefighters Calendar." Maddie leaned up and put her hands on the back of Britt's seat. "You could never disappoint anyone."

"Believe me, I have."

Both girls made sounds of disbelief. "Like when?" Britt asked.

He skipped over his rotten marriage and parenting skills that along with nudges from Jenny's mother had caused the breakup between them. "When I was a teenager, my mom and dad were disappointed in me more often than they weren't."

"Grandma and Grandpa, mad at you?" Maddie said. "Why?"

"A few times for making bad grades, sometimes for sneaking out when I was supposed to be in my room studying."

Neither girl commented. Interesting, but what would they say, other than to deny they'd ever done anything like that? He knew Maddie had. "I want you to know, Maddie, that I didn't like history classes myself. Trust me, it's good to be aware of what happened in the past, both here and in the world."

"Whatever," she muttered and sat back. "Why did you sneak out?"

Mostly to be with Jenny when they wanted to be alone. Not about to get into that, he bypassed the question. "I may have skipped a class or two, but not often enough to get a school counselor or one of my teachers involved."

"You were smart, Dad."

"Maybe, but by skipping class, I missed out on learning things that are important."

"So you're saying don't cut class and do my homework."

"You got it."

"I like my classes," Britt said. "Also, I don't want Mom bugging me."

"She makes me so mad," Maddie grumbled. "She's been upset since I got home from school Tuesday and acts like she still is."

"Yeah," Britt chimed in. "Even though I'm not the one she's mad at, it's been hard to be in the house with her."

Rob could relate. If Jenny was mad or unhappy, everyone she loved suffered. "When your mom acts like that, it's because she's worried about you. You'd feel worse if she didn't care at all." He pulled up the gravel drive of his modest one-story. He and Jenny lived a scant mile and a half from each other in vastly different houses.

"You don't do that, Dad. If you're mad, you tell us and get over it."

He couldn't think what to say to that. The girls let themselves out of the car, grabbed their stuff, and headed for the front door. He followed.

Alcatraz, named because as a pup he acted like a wily convict, sneaking food from the table or counter and hiding it around the house, heard their voices and barked joyously as soon as they walked through the door. The collie was hard to resist, and he knew it. Both girls immediately lightened up. Rob relaxed. "He sure loves you two. Put your stuff in your room while I give him his dinner. Then, it'll be time to get you two fed."

"Speaking of dinner ..." Maddie widened her eyes. "Can we go to Harvey's for pizza? We'll do our homework as soon as we get home—promise."

Best pizza place in town, even if it was at the south end and a good twenty-minute drive away. Rob grinned. "So that's the reason you wanted to come over." If saying yes to that meant he was a pushover, so be it. "Sure."

~

As MADDIE and Britt unpacked in the bedroom they shared at their dad's house, Maddie talked to her twin in a low voice he couldn't hear. "Guess what I saw when I came out after the review and went to meet Mom and Dad at the car? They were holding hands!"

"No way!" Britt started to squeal, but Maddie shushed her.

"We're not supposed to know."

"Do you think they might really like each other?"

"It sure looks that way."

"That'd be so dope."

"Right? You almost told Mom about Hudson," she said, shooting Britt a dirty look. "Promise you won't tell her or Dad about us."

"Why would I do that? You can't tell them about Theo, either. They don't need to know you didn't stay at Mr. Mister the other day. You never should've skipped class to be with him. That's what got you in trouble."

"How else are we supposed to be alone together? He has football practice and a part-time job bagging groceries. That doesn't give us much time for anything."

"Being alone isn't that hard," Britt said. "Next time, try what Theo and I did the other day. We got our food and had a picnic at one of those tables along the trail in the woods. No one goes this time of year, and we were all by ourselves. None of our friends care. We all want our alone time."

"I know that, Britt, but Hudson and I need more

than a thirty-minute lunch break to ourselves. And don't tell me to sneak out. Mom has ways of knowing stuff, almost like she spies on us. Why can't she be okay with us staying out later?" she grumbled as she unpacked. Their curfews were ridiculously early. "I wish she'd trust us."

"You know why—she's scared we'll get pregnant like she did."

Maddie was horrified. "As if! We're not stupid. We know how to be safe."

Her sister squinted at her. "Are you and Hudson doing it?"

"Not yet, but we might. You?"

Britt shook her head. "I'm not ready, and neither is Theo. I hope you pass your World History test next week."

"I'm going to try."

"Forget trying. Do it, okay? So you can use your phone and iPad again."

"You two about done unpacking?" their dad called out from down the hall. "I'm hungry and you need time after dinner to do your homework."

"Be right there," Britt replied, as she and Maddie choked back laughter.

Having a sister like Britt was the best.

4

An extra free night without the kids! Jenny couldn't believe her luck. Her thoughts went immediately to Shawn. A successful insurance agent, he'd be attending an insurance conference in San Francisco from tomorrow through the following week, and she wouldn't see him for a while. But with the evening just beginning ...

Standing in the hallway, she phoned him right away. "Hey, I know this is spur of the moment, and you're probably packing for your trip and taking care of whatever else needs doing before you fly out in the morning," she began when he answered. "That leaves tonight free, right? Good news—Rob took the kids a day early, so if you're not busy ..."

"To see you? I'm wide open. My flight leaves at eight tomorrow, which means I'll be getting up early. Okay if I stay over?"

Why not? "That works for me. I switched my Monday meeting at Fashion Dogs to tomorrow. It starts at nine."

"Great. I'm almost finished packing, then I'll head over. What'll we do about dinner?"

She hadn't planned to cook, had decided she and

the girls would eat leftovers. Going out seemed a good idea. "You choose—I'm open to anywhere."

"Pizza at Harvey's. Pick you up in thirty."

ON THE WAY to Harvey's, the girls talked about the pies they would order. Being the best pizza joint in town, the place was bustling. Not quite as busy as it would be Friday and Saturday nights, but a fair crowd for a Thursday. Rob didn't mind the noise and chaos and neither did the girls. To his surprise, Gus, Max, Adam, and Nate, four of his crewmates, were seated around a table, sharing a pitcher and munching snacks while they waited for their orders.

Living together forty-eight hours straight each week and watching each other's backs during fires and medical calls had bonded them tighter than most people ever got. Always happy to see any of his crewmates, Rob greeted them, then nodded at his daughters. "Brought some special people with me."

Smiles all around. The guys had known the twins since birth and welcomed them like royalty, which of course, they loved. After the tension at Jenny's, it was a relief to see them light up and be more like their usual selves.

"You two have grown since I last saw you," Nate said, his voice loud to be heard over the noise. "Why don't you join us and catch us up on things?"

"Can we, Dad?" Britt asked. Rob nodded and helped Max and Nate scrounge up three empty chairs and bring them over.

Hard not to notice the attention he and his crewmates attracted. Thanks to the calendar, everyone recognized them. Heads turned, customers waved, and a few women threw them sultry looks. Most of the guys were either seeing someone or married, but they'd grown used to the attention. Knowing the importance of projecting good will, which was good PR, they smiled and nodded in return.

Maddie and Britt were too busy taking their seats and chatting with their tablemates to pay any attention to the envious looks diners gave them. They were enjoying their pizzas and conversation when Maddie squinted toward the entrance. "OMG, Mom just walked in. With *Shawn*." She made a face. "What're they doing here?"

Rob wondered the same thing. His buds turned their heads and checked out Jenny's date.

"Jenny," Nate called out. She started toward them, then caught sight of Rob and the girls and stopped in her tracks.

"That a new boyfriend?" Adam asked.

Jenny claimed he wasn't her boyfriend, but Rob knew better. "Yep." He didn't care much for Shawn and didn't hide his dislike. Jenny had accused him of making negative assumptions about the man he'd only met once, but he had his reasons. The guy was way too full of himself and made sure everyone knew he was the coolest and most successful insurance agent in town.

He expected Jenny to walk on by. Instead, she headed straight for the table, leaving Shawn behind. She threw Rob a seriously annoyed frown. "What are you and the girls doing here?"

"We have to eat, don't we? We're enjoying our dinner." Or were. "Same question to you."

Shawn joined her in time to answer, "We're hungry."

Now Rob understood why she'd agreed so readily

to let the girls stay with him an extra night. "Hey, Shawn," he grumbled. The insurance agent was an inch or so shorter than Rob's six foot-one. With the tip of his nose turned up slightly and a toothy smile, some would call him good-looking. Rob thought otherwise.

"Hi," Jenny's date returned, flashing a quick, fake smile.

"Meet Shawn," she told the guys.

Every man in the crew liked her, and five trusted her with their dogs. They gave her an enthusiastic hello. Their responses to her date were more subdued. The twins avoided looking at their mother or her boyfriend, their matching clamped lips and slightly narrowed eyes speaking volumes.

"I want to leave, Dad," Maddie suddenly announced. "Can we take the leftovers home?"

He shot Britt a questioning look. "I still have homework to finish," she said. "We both do."

Fine with him. "Okay. Hang on, while I get boxes for us and settle up."

Jenny followed him to the order counter and crossed her arms. "It's like you're rewarding Maddie, and after I grounded her. On a school night, too. They should be at your house doing their homework."

He resented the judgment. "Maddie's being punished, and you know it—you saw to that. I brought them here because I hadn't planned to cook, and they like the pizza. They'll do their schoolwork when we get home, so get off my case."

She got right up in his face. "Don't you dare talk to me like that. You bent the rules."

Like him, she seemed to have forgotten how to be civil. "No, they wanted something for dinner and I brought them here. So sue me. They enjoyed visiting with the guys, but they're not happy to see you with

Shawn." Neither was Rob, even if the men she dated weren't his business.

"He's a nice guy," Jenny said through her teeth. "Which you'd realize if you had an ounce of the manners your mother taught you and got to know him a little."

He hid the sting of the comment under a scoff. "Tell that to the girls."

"We already discussed this, Rob. They're fifteen and don't want to share me with him. As we also mentioned, they're just as unhappy when you're dating someone. They were especially upset when you moved in with Nora."

Rob remembered. Before long, he'd felt the same way. "That was a couple of years ago, and they were right about her." Moving in together had been a big mistake, not on a par with his doomed marriage, but unhappy enough. It'd be a long time, if ever, before he tried that again. "What does that have to do with Shawn?"

Jenny's face reddened, a sure sign she was on the verge of losing her temper even more than she had. He was, too, he realized and backtracked. "We shouldn't be doing this here or any place where the girls and our friends are. We're leaving shortly."

"You'd better be," she muttered.

Having had enough of her hostile cracks, he pivoted away to pay the tab. By the time he collected the boxes and brought them to the table, Jenny and Shawn had moved out of his line of vision.

His crewmates were chatting with the twins, doing what they could to keep them distracted. It hadn't worked—they were all eyes and frowns as they glanced Jenny's way. It was obvious they'd noticed the less-than-friendly conversation between them, even if it was too noisy to hear anything. He felt like crap for losing his cool in public.

"You two okay?" he asked as they headed for the car.

"Uh-uh," Britt said. "We don't like Shawn." That made three of them. "I thought you and mom were getting back together, but I guess not."

Say what? He frowned. "Where'd you get that crazy idea?"

"Maddie said—"

"Let me tell him, Britt. I saw you holding hands after my review class earlier."

Jenny would blow her stack when she heard about that. "Does it look like we're getting together?" he said, with an irritated *pfft*. "As your mom already explained to Maddie, we didn't want to keep you waiting. She's not a fast runner, I helped her along. That's it."

Neither twin said anything. With their unhappy expressions, they didn't need to. Great, now they were all in bad moods. Working to change that, he took them to Carleton's, a new bakery in town, and bought cookies for the three of them. Then he took them home.

5

R ob and the girls left the pizzeria, and as Jenny headed toward the small corner table Shawn had found during her confrontation with her former spouse, her temper continued to sizzle. He was so infuriating! Did he have to give Shawn the cold shoulder? "I apologize for my ex," she said as soon as she joined him. It was a relief to be on the opposite side of the room and away from the firefighters.

"I don't blame the guy. If I were in his shoes, I'd react the same way."

Mild-mannered Shawn? "Would you, though?"

"No, but only because I'm trained to be friendly at all times."

"Rob and I have been divorced thirteen years, and we've gone our separate ways. It's long past time he moved on."

"Are you sure *you* have?"

Jenny couldn't believe he'd ask and was super annoyed. "Come on, Shawn, I did that ages ago."

"Your kids sure don't think much of me."

True. "They really don't know you. I agree, they were upset to see me with you tonight, but don't let it bother you. They're full of hormones and overly emotional—all fifteen-year-old girls are."

"I'll bet they'd be smiling if you and your ex got back together."

"Then they're in for a lifetime of disappointment. That will never, ever happen. We're both free to date other people, and we both do. But he's the one with the surly behavior and negative opinions." Yet even as she voiced the words, she silently admitted feeling out-of-sorts when he dated someone for more than a few weeks. So, yes, she understood where he was coming from. At least she had the decency to hide her feelings.

"You were as unhappy to see Rob and your kids tonight as they were to see me."

Also true. "The way they snubbed us? So rude. I didn't expect to see them, either, but I wasn't going to give anyone the cold shoulder." Yet running into them and tussling with her ex had ruined the evening. Losing her temper in front of them and everyone had made it all worse. "I'm not hungry anymore, Shawn. I want to go home."

"No problem. I'll ask for our pizza to be divided in half and put in separate boxes."

It sounded like he wasn't staying the night, or even planning to stop at her house for long. She didn't care enough to ask. He no longer seemed right for her. A shock, but not really. She'd tried hard to fall for him, but it hadn't happened. "I'll split the bill with you."

"Not necessary."

Before long, boxes in hand, they were in Shawn's Lexus and headed for her house. The ride was mostly silent until he pulled into her driveway and braked to a stop. "I like you, Jenny, but this isn't working. I don't think we should see each other again."

She'd been about to say the same thing. "I agree, and I'm sorry because I like you, too. No hard feelings, okay? It was fun while it lasted."

"It was never as relaxed as I thought it would be, not with us tiptoeing around your daughters. We mostly got together when they weren't home."

"You saw how they behaved tonight. Imagine them acting like that every time we went out. I've worked hard to teach them manners, but at times they don't care. For that, I apologize."

"Maybe if they'd had a chance to know me better, they'd have accepted me—us."

As she'd told Rob, she doubted they'd ever warm to Shawn or any other man. She needed to work on that with them, have a heart-to-heart about wanting to date and meet someone she wanted a future with. As if. They'd battle her every step of the way. Not sure how to respond, she sighed. "You can't possibly get it —you don't have children."

"I know enough to understand when a woman's interests are focused on someone else."

She frowned. "Such as?"

"Your ex."

She gaped at him. "You've got to be kidding me. We can't even be in the same room for more than ten minutes without upsetting each other. You saw that tonight."

"I certainly did. I'm no therapist, but my guess is you two fight because you still care about each other and don't know what to do about it."

The mildly-uttered words—did he never get angry or upset?—hit hard somewhere in Jenny's gut, but she wasn't sure why it galled her. Except that his words rang false. Right? Of course, they did. Not an ounce of truth to them. She may have had a moment walking around the school grounds with Rob, but that was due to nostalgia long past its prime and had quickly passed. Even then, they'd argued about a few things. Running across the football field with him holding her hand didn't mean anything. Not after all this time.

Her unexpected, misplaced confusion was Shawn's fault. How dare he presume to tell her what she felt when he had no idea what he was talking about? "You're way off base," she told him without an ounce of warmth. "It's a darn good thing you're not a therapist. You'd make a lousy one."

Still too easy-going for the serious tone of their conversation, he shrugged one shoulder. "I call it the way I see it. I'll grab the suitcase I left in the living room, then go home and get some sleep." He was in and out in under a minute. "Goodbye, Jenny. I hope you find what you're looking for."

It wasn't Shawn. What had she ever seen in him? "Goodbye." She locked the door behind her.

≈

JENNY ENJOYED MEETING weekly with the talented women at Fashion Dogs. They reviewed the previous week's numbers and discussed plans for the week ahead. She preferred Mondays, but had switched this one to Friday. Which turned out to be great timing.

This morning, she especially looked forward to spending time with her staff and welcomed the chance to forget about the disastrous previous evening at Harvey's. What better way to distract herself than an hour with the talented women who truly enjoyed their work? They took up the second floor of the modest building she rented. Three did the sewing on the machines designed specifically for canine clothing, and one managed operations, orders, and shipping. Thanks to them and Paula, the fifth employee and a social media whiz who updated the website and worked from home, the business ran smoothly.

As always, Jenny brought treats and coffee to the meeting. "I spoke with our accountant earlier in the week and have great news," she told them. "We continue to grow. The doggie Halloween outfits are selling well, and so are the Thanksgiving and Christmas orders. Third quarter was our best ever, and with the holidays in full swing we should have our best year to date. Keep up the good work."

They all seemed pleased.

Wendy, the forty-year-old operations manager, signaled she wanted to say something. "We're all working hard. It'd be great if there were more of us."

Jenny agreed. "That reminds me, I hired two of the temps we used last year to work through the holidays. They'll be here Monday morning, and if all goes well, I'll bring them in on a more permanent basis. Don't think I haven't noticed how hard you're working. You'll all be getting nice year-end bonuses."

The women cheered. It was nice to be appreciated, and she went home smiling.

Alicia was waiting to take the dogs out for their walks. After several years working together, Jenny liked her a great deal and trusted her, too. Even though she was about eight years younger than Jenny, they never ran out of things to talk about. She shared things with Alicia she didn't dare tell her girlfriends from the firehouse, mainly because there was no guarantee they'd be able to keep what, if anything, was happening with her and Rob private. Today though, she studiously avoided mentioning the fiasco at Harvey's. She was too upset, and it was too soon to talk about that. When Alicia left several hours later, so did any trace of Jenny's good mood.

6

A s Friday wore on, Jenny grew more and more upset about the atrocious manners of Rob and the twins. By midafternoon, tired of her own company, she reached out to Wanda and Hallie, two of her favorite people, and invited them to join her for dinner and drinks at Mama's Cantina on the west side of town. Both were in serious relationships with two of Rob's crewmates—Wanda with Gus and Hallie with Owen. They immediately agreed to meet up, as this being a Friday night, their partners and other firefighters were at the standing Friday-night poker game. Having the twins for the weekend, Rob had skipped it.

They arrived at the restaurant within minutes of each other. Intent on relaxing and enjoying the evening, Jenny decided to steer clear of any mention of Harvey's.

"How's business?" Hallie asked after they ordered drinks and nacho appetizers.

"The dog boarding/walking side of my life is doing well. Business at Fashion Dogs is fantastic."

Her friends congratulated her and talked about their jobs. Hallie was a freelance writer, and Wanda had recently bought the hair and nail salon where she worked.

Talk soon turned in a different direction. "How's Shawn?" Wanda asked. "Do I ever get to meet him?"

"I'm not seeing him anymore. We broke up last night."

"What?" Her friend's eyes widened. "You so liked him."

"As it turned out, not that much."

"You talked about him like you did. What changed? Was it because of what happened at Harvey's?"

Should've known they'd find out. It was a sure bet the guys at the firehouse and every other employee at GLFD had heard about it.

Yet, her friends had caught her by surprise. She frowned. "You know about that and didn't think to mention it?"

For a moment, neither of them replied. Then Hallie sighed. "We were waiting for you to bring it up. What happened?"

"It's kind of a long story, and I don't want to bore you."

"I think I can speak for both Hallie and me when I say we're all ears."

"Fire away," Hallie agreed, then grinned at herself. "I made a pun without even trying."

"A really bad one," Jenny groaned, and the three of them broke into laughter. She couldn't remember the last time she'd enjoyed a genuine laugh. It felt good. The two friends were fun to be with, exactly what she needed.

Between that and a fair amount of the margarita she'd sipped loosening her tongue, she went straight to the story. She filled them in about Maddie and the review class she'd taken, leaving out the part about holding hands with Rob because it'd been a necessity and didn't matter, then moved on. "The girls wanted to stay with Rob Thursday night, so I let them. I had an unexpected free evening and was excited about it. Before Shawn and I knew we were breaking up, we decided to eat at Harvey's."

Wanda leaned forward. "I hadn't heard about that."

Both friends licked their lips in anticipation, more fodder for the firehouse mill. No sense worrying about that now. Jenny continued. "From the second we walked in and saw Rob and the girls, things got," she paused to think, "let's call them unpleasant." She talked about the girls' hostility and Rob's rudeness toward Shawn, then moved on to the argument she'd had with Rob, which the girls, crew members who were there, and anyone interested in what was happening between her and Rob, watched them both unravel.

"I spent almost a year in therapy. One of the things I learned was how to manage my temper around Rob. Last night, I forgot all that. He went through therapy, too, and he wasn't any better. Due to the noise, no one could hear what we said, but they got the gist. Everyone was upset, especially Maddie and Britt. Rob took them back to his house. I hate that they saw all that. They weren't the only ones affected." Thinking about it now, Jenny got angry all over again, so much so that her hands trembled. "Shawn and I were too upset to stay, and we left, too."

Her friends exchanged looks. "That we know," Wanda said. "But we want the details."

Jenny gaped at them. "You heard about that, too?"

"From Gus and Owen," Halley told her. "They

were there, remember? As their better halves, they had to fill us in. The whole thing sounds like a nightmare, but what does it have to do with you and Shawn breaking up? Don't tell me you two also got into an argument."

"Not at all. My ex is the only male I fight with and rarely these days. Any disagreements are done in private. But not last night. Back to Shawn and me. The decision to split up was mutual. I was relieved, and he didn't seem the slightest bit upset, either. He never even frowned. It was like we were discussing the weather."

"Ah." Wanda gave a knowing nod. "There's no spark between you. I never saw you together, and you never said anything, so I had no idea."

"The sex was okay, but not fabulous," Jenny admitted. "On the plus side, he seemed like someone I could be with for a long time, maybe even marriage material. We got along well and liked a lot of the same things. I realize now that there's more to life than getting along. For a man with his drive and smarts, he's as dull as a faded dog leash. I don't know what I ever saw in him.

"Rob had no idea about any of that. For no reason at all, he was incredibly rude to Shawn. That's why I lost it and lit into him. I'm still steamed about it. But did I have to go public about it? I so regret acting the way I did in front of the girls and everyone else. I'd give anything if they hadn't been there. Sometimes I wonder how they can stand me."

"Come on," Hallie said. "Everyone knows you're a great mom, including your daughters."

"I don't know about that. Sometimes I overdo the scolding, and I'm not very forgiving." Rob was right about that and the way she disregarded his opinions on how to deal with the various issues that came up with the girls.

So many bad habits learned from her mother. Growing up, she'd rebelled against some of the same things in her own teenage passive-aggressive way. Therapy had helped tremendously, although she'd waited till after her mother had died to see a therapist. Why? Because dear old Mom believed therapy wasn't for Jenny, that as a strong woman, she didn't need help from anyone. Big joke—she'd *really* needed it.

Thanks to counseling, she'd let go of many of the misbeliefs her mother had saddled her with. Apparently, not all of them. Here she was, continuing the cycle of repeatedly lecturing Maddie and sometimes Britt when repetition didn't do any good. Still, despite what Rob might think, she wasn't nearly as rigid as her mother had been.

"The girls are at the age where everything I do is wrong," she added. "They don't feel that way about Rob. I'm the bad guy and he's Mr. Awesome. So unfair." She let out a frustrated breath. "Last night, I reinforced my bad-guy image."

Wanda's speculative expression bothered Jenny. "What's with the knowing look?"

"I think maybe there's still something between you two."

Jenny ignored both women's uh-huh nods. "Of course, there is. The twins and Alcatraz."

"You know what we mean."

"Now you sound like Shawn," she said and rolled her eyes.

Hallie frowned. "Huh?"

"He had the gall to suggest that Rob and I got into it last night because we still have feelings for each other and don't know what to do with them. Can you believe it?"

After tapping a thoughtful finger to her lips, Hallie commented. "I find that very interesting."

"Well, stop. It's not true, and I mean it."

Wanda cast an equally doubtful expression her way. "If you say so."

As she didn't seem convinced, Jenny was compelled to repeat herself. "Rob and I don't feel that way about each other, okay? When people think otherwise, it's upsetting."

"How many people are we talking about?"

"You two and Shawn, for starters."

"There must be some truth to it," Wanda said. "Otherwise, you'd shrug it off."

Fed up with the direction of the conversation, Jenny tightened her lips. "Can we please stop talking about it? Right now, what I'm interested in is how to get back on track with Rob. It's important that we get along. Any ideas?"

"Therapy-wise, you might consider a touch-up," Wanda said. "Together this time."

Something to think about, but Jenny was well-versed on her therapist's ideas. Plus, going through therapy with Rob, revisiting the past and all that, sounded like torture. "I'm not sure I want to do that. Any other suggestions?"

Her two friends looked thoughtful, then Hallie shook her head. "None that I can think of."

Wanda opened her mouth to say who knew what, when at that moment, the server delivered the meals. Perfect timing. They spent the rest of the evening eating, laughing, and enjoying each other.

Jenny left in a good mood. But on the drive home, she mulled over the ridiculous idea that she and Rob still cared about each other and had unresolved feelings. Those who believed it were wrong. What mattered was to get back to where they'd been and be nice to each other again.

~

When Jenny woke up Sunday morning, her first thought was to talk with Rob about the other night and figure out the next steps to avoiding anything close to a repeat. She intended to talk to him about it when he dropped off the girls and Alcatraz later that afternoon. And be civil, too, if it killed her.

One thing was certain: they both needed to relax, something neither of them did very well. Meanwhile, she made a list of activities and exercises to help with that. There were plenty of suggestions online: massage therapy—an activity she strongly approved of—brisk walks without the dogs, soothing cups of tea. Breathing, meditation, mindfulness, yoga, soothing music, laughing often, getting enough sleep. So many options.

She texted her ex. *Can we talk alone when you bring the girls and Alcatraz over?*

A few minutes later, he replied with a thumbs-up emoji.

That was the sum total of his text but then, she hadn't shared any specifics. If the conversation didn't go well? Couples therapy, she guessed. Otherwise, they might stop talking at all.

7

Rob read Jenny's text and scratched his head. What was it this time? She'd already bawled him out for giving Shawn the cold shoulder the other night. Whatever it was, he had no interest in accusations or lectures. He was steamed enough about the argument she'd come at him with the other night, and in front of all those people. The girls had been so upset. Irritation ate at him the entire weekend. By the time he hustled the girls and Alcatraz into the Subaru to drive to Jenny's late Sunday afternoon, he was in no mood to deal with whatever she'd put on the agenda. But for his daughters' sakes, he'd tread softly and work at avoiding a run-in.

"Do we have to go back to Mom's house?" Maddie whined as he started the car.

"You know we do," he said, although he understood the dread.

"We want to stay with you," Britt agreed.

Oh, man, Jenny would have fits over that. He pushed his self-concerns aside for now. "Do that, and you'll break your mom's heart. She loves you both so much."

"She doesn't act like it. She's always mad at us," Maddie complained. "Always."

Teenage girls could be so dramatic. If he hadn't been driving, he'd have rolled his eyes. "That's not true, and you know it. There are plenty of times when you have fun together."

"You don't want us to stay with you." She sounded hurt.

Not possible with his schedule. "You know how much I'd enjoy that. But I work from eight a.m. to eight a.m. forty-eight hours straight. And don't forget the auto-detailing business when I'm off shift. You'd be at your mom's house all the time while I worked, just like now."

"It's not fair."

"Fair or not, it's the way things are."

With winter coming, darkness fell earlier by the day. When he pulled up Jenny's driveway, dusk had fallen. Motion detector lights illuminated the walkway leading to the front door. The drapes were closed, but light escaped through spaces both on the main floor and upstairs, where the bedrooms and a bathroom were located. Lit up as it was, the house was the picture of cozy and welcoming. Not for him, it wasn't.

Damn, there went his be-careful meter.

Oblivious, Alcatraz yipped happily, his wagging tail visible in the growing darkness. The pooch loved Jenny as much as she loved him. Easy to do, when she treated him so well. She must've been watching for them—she opened the door before they reached the front stoop with a warm smile directed at the twins. "I'm so glad to see you two. And you, too, Alcatraz."

Both girls looked surprised. "You're not mad at us anymore?" Britt asked.

"I didn't say that. You're still grounded, Maddie.

But if you pass the test with a C or higher, we're good to go."

Maddie's exaggerated huff said what she thought of the idea. "So you've said a million times, Mom."

"Did you finish your homework?" They both nodded. "Great. Please put your things away while I talk to your dad."

The girls glanced at each other, then quickly disappeared up the stairs with their weekenders. Rob didn't intend to stay long, as he wanted to get home and chill before starting his shift in the morning. Bracing himself for who knew what, he shoved his hands in his jeans pockets, thumbs out. "Let's get this over with. How did I screw up this time?"

"Please, Rob, I want us to get along."

Like she had last night? In an effort to keep things cordial, he bit back the sarcastic question and sniffed the air. "Something smells good."

"Beef stew—my mother's recipe." His stomach rumbled. "I made plenty, and if you want to stay ..."

This wasn't at all what he'd expected. He eyed her. "You're inviting me to dinner?"

"Don't look so surprised. You had the girls for three nights. It's the least I can do."

"Yeah, but the other night at Harvey's—"

"You were hostile to Shawn, a bad lesson in courtesy for the girls, but that's not what this is about. I'm sorry I argued with you, let alone in public. I feel like we slid backwards to when we were always at each other's throats. Can we go back to where we were before that night and agree not to do that ever again in front of anyone?"

The great thing about Jenny, which he'd forgotten till now because it hadn't happened since their fighting days way back when, was that after she had time to process stuff, she often apologized. He forgave her instantly, almost wanted to pull her close and kiss her. Forget that. Brain blip, that was all. "It's behind us now."

"Oh, good. Hallie and Wanda know about the other night, of course. They suggested touch-up therapy or maybe a couple's thing, but I don't want to do that. Do you?"

He had no interest in going back in time yet again, especially with her. "Not particularly. What do you think we should do?"

"Find a way to reduce the tension I seem to have. You're every bit as tense."

He didn't disagree. "It's true."

"We each have a lot on our plates. If we can both just relax ... I've been researching ways to stay balanced and calm, things like deep breathing, massage, soothing music, yoga, exercise, and so on. Do any of those appeal to you?"

He wasn't going to bring up Jenny's boyfriend, but it happened. "What does Shawn have to say about us? Does he think we need to be more easy-going?"

Her compressed lips said it all. *You don't get to ask.* His temper started to rise, but she was right. Besides, he was as sorry about the other night as she was and meant to be civilized. He tried a different tack. "Something going on with you and him?" he probed, keeping his tone neutral and calm.

"I guess you could say that."

"I'm sure you two will work it out."

"Oh, we did. We broke up."

"Huh." Some of the tension inside dissipated, not because he cared who she dated, but because he didn't like Shawn. "You okay about that?"

She nodded "It was the right thing to do."

"Because the girls don't like him," he figured.

"That had nothing to do with the decision. They have to get used to me dating."

As did Rob, although after all this time he still hadn't. It wasn't his fault she picked guys who weren't right for her. None of his business, but he was entitled to his opinions. "What happened?"

"It was a mutual agreement."

It was clear she had nothing more to say about it. Fine with him. Out of nowhere and for the second time since he'd walked through the door, he wanted to hug her. She looked at him like she might want that, too. Especially with her cheeks suddenly flushed.

Time to leave. As he reached for his coat, she spoke. "What are we going to do to keep our cool? Let's pick an option and try it."

"I'll think about that and get back to you when I pick up Alcatraz Wednesday."

"Then you're not staying for dinner." She didn't seem to mind at all.

He shook his head. "Thanks, but I need to get home and enjoy a night of solitude."

"I understand."

"I know you do."

They actually smiled at each other. Much better— safer—than a hug, which was way out of line.

"Do you want to say goodbye to the girls before you leave?"

"I always do. I'll go upstairs and tell them now."

～

IT WAS standard practice that mornings at the firehouse started with breakfasts each teammate supplied himself, followed by mandatory equipment and inventory checks on the two fire engines and the aid cars, which, unlike ambulances, were used to provide emergency medical response at the location without transporting them. After breakfast Monday, Rob and a few other crewmates tromped downstairs to the apparatus bay, aka the garage. He was paired with Gus, and while they checked off items on the chores list, they talked about things that hadn't come up at breakfast.

"Man, that night at Harvey's was rough," Gus said. "For a while there, I thought sure you and Jenny would tear each other apart."

Rob felt sheepish. "Shouldn't have happened," he said by way of apologizing.

After inspection ended and all supplies had been replenished and equipment returned to where it belonged, they headed upstairs for the weekly required physical fitness workout—time allowing, most everyone trained more than once a week. The conversation continued. "There are times when Jenny pushes all my buttons, especially when she accuses me of stuff I haven't done," Rob said. "She claimed I was rude to Shawn."

"You were, man."

Rob glanced down and thought a moment. "I guess so. Something about the guy rubs me the wrong way."

"That's an easy one. It's because he's with Jenny."

He couldn't argue with that but didn't want the guy to think he had a thing for his ex. He didn't. Even if he had been thinking about his weird urges to hold her. "He strikes me as a phony, like he's hiding his true self. Gives me a bad taste."

"Like when a matador waves a red cape at a bull."

"It's not like that. I don't care for the man, okay?"

"I'd go bonkers if I saw Wanda anywhere with a new guy."

Perfect segue. "So, when I dropped the dog and twins at Jenny's last night, she hits me with two things —first, that she and Shawn broke up, and second, she thinks we should find a class or something to help us relax."

"Couples fight. Everyone does. I don't know what to say. You'll figure it out." Gus shrugged his massive shoulders and nodded toward the gym. "Ready to do this?"

"Bring it."

Sometime later, after a grueling workout that felt great, they all showered.

By then, it was almost lunchtime. "Slow day," Rob said.

Tony, another crewmate, put his finger to his lips as in *shh*. "Don't jinx it. Let's enjoy it while it lasts."

They headed to the kitchen with their lunches and talked sports and whatever else was on their minds.

"Hey, Rob," Daniel said. "I heard you and Jenny got into it at Harvey's the other night."

Rob grimaced. "Who told you?"

"I did," Adam said. "It's not a situation a guy can easily forget."

Lately, Rob had heard that way too many times. "I'm aware of that. Jenny and I don't fight like that anymore, especially in front of the kids. Neither of us is happy about that. At least it was too noisy in there for anyone to hear what we said."

"No need to hear the words. Your faces and body language did all the talking."

"What *did* you say?" Tony wanted to know.

In no mood to rehash the thing, Rob collected what was left of his lunch and stood. "I'm—"

A call from Sarah McCone, the daytime dispatch operator interrupted him and signaled a fire.

The crew headed downstairs at a fast clip, where they quickly donned their turnout gear and steel-toe boots. Then, decked out and ready, they jumped into the big fire engine.

Liam, one of the engineers, drove. Rob rode up front with him. Liam wore a microphone headset and listened closely to the dispatcher. "Ten-four." A minute later, he told Rob to keep an eye out for unexpected obstacles in the way.

Rob directed him around a construction blockage on one road and let him know when to turn.

"Where are we headed?" Daniel wanted to know.

"A warehouse in the industrial area, way on the south end."

"Warehouse fire?" Daniel swore.

Everyone felt the same about that. No telling what they'd find. Things got quiet, guys focused on getting there and getting the job done.

"Cooper's Flocking," Rob mused as they pulled into the parking lot of the warehouse. He didn't know much about flocking, except that it involved placing tiny fibers on an adhesive-coated surface and that the stuff was fire-retardant but not fire-resistant.

Ahead of them, a group of men and women, several aid cars, and two police vehicles had arrived. The engine pulled up close to the building. Inside, a propane-powered lift truck had caught fire due to a fuel system fitting that'd come loose. The operator jumped off the truck, saving his life as they all watched it roll into a storage area of baled flock and rags, and ignite.

It was a dangerous situation and took hours to subdue and finally extinguish. The building had sustained extensive damage. By the time the crew finished and moved outside to talk with senior management, the police, and other officials and news media who showed up, it was late afternoon. At some point, an ambulance had left with a critically burned employee. Two additional ambulances had transported others to the same hospital for less serious burns and/or treatment of smoke inhalation. Considering the severity of the fire, it was amazing that more people weren't injured.

Rob and the entire crew were exhausted, but they were all in one piece. On the drive back, conversation was minimal. They were too drained to talk much. Parts of Rob's body, namely his legs, arms, and lower back ached from the extreme exertion the fire had put him through.

After showering, they gathered in the kitchen for the evening meal. It was Ethan's night to cook. Rob was glad it wasn't his. Somehow, the guy cooked up a delicious, hearty soup, exactly what he needed. After chowing down two helpings of everything, his belly finally filled up. Liam and Hank had clean-up duty. Wanting something sweet, but too worn out to go far, Rob trekked to Macgregor Drugs, a small drugstore two blocks from the station, and bought several packages of cookies.

On the way back, he opened one and polished off one of the sleeves. Some of the guys had returned to the dining room and were playing a board game. Others were busy with their cellphones. "Who wants cookies?" he said, holding up the packages.

Thanks chorused through the room as crewmates gathered around the goods and stuffed their faces just as he had.

"My pleasure," he said. "I'm turning in."

After crawling into bed, he phoned Jenny. He needed to talk to someone about the fire and she was it.

"Hey," she said. "What's up?"

"Brutal warehouse fire this afternoon." He shared the details and ended with, "I'm beat and every muscle in my body aches."

"You poor man."

When she was sweet like now, he enjoyed talking to her. "I'll live. Before I forget, I think Maddie and Britt listened in to part of our conversation last night."

"But they were upstairs."

"They must've stood on the stairs and eavesdropped."

"Little sneaks. What makes you think so?"

"Their less-than-pleased expressions, like they thought I should've accepted the dinner invitation. Guess it's my turn to upset them. How are they doing?"

"Pretty well. Maddie's studying a lot for that test. She really wants to do well and get off restriction."

"Fingers crossed. How's Britt?"

"She seems fine."

"I'm too tired to talk to them tonight, but give them air kisses from me. At their age, that's about all they can tolerate. If they look unhappy, I'll know they're mad at me."

"Come on, to them you're the good parent, and you can do no wrong. But I'll watch their faces and text you. I'm really eager for us to get along like we were. Do any of the ideas I mentioned last night appeal to you?"

"I haven't had time to think about it. I'm open to any of them. Which one are you leaning toward?"

"Hmm ... You're sore and tense. I'm tense, too.

We're both stressed out from work, the kids, and who knows what else. Why don't I schedule massages for us at the same time? Afterward, we can test out our ability to get along when the tension isn't there. The results won't last, but at least we'll find out if being relaxed has a positive effect on our relationship. Yes or no?"

Seemed a silly idea, but how would he know when he'd never indulged in a massage. "I'm game. Where exactly would it be?"

"The Massage Plus Spa at Guff's Lake Resort. When I turned thirty, some of my friends gave me a gift card there. It was truly wonderful. We can split the cost."

The resort, which was part of the Guff's Lake Park, was about fifteen miles from the GLFD and half that from the neighborhood where they lived. "Fine by me."

"I'll ask Frankie, a part-time assistant I use from time to time—you've met her— to help Alicia with the dogs. I'll set the massage for Wednesday, late morning, if that works for you."

She sounded really stoked about it, and his sore body needed help. "For sure. I'll pick you up."

"Great. Get a good night's sleep."

"I intend to, unless there's another fire call tonight."

"Perish the thought. I'll let you go."

Moments after disconnecting, he passed out.

8

I n an unusually upbeat mood Tuesday morning, Jenny booked massages for her and Rob for the following day. She so looked forward to an hour of TLC and knew Rob would like it, too. She texted him to let him know. *Hope you slept well last night. Appointment begins tomorrow at 10:00. You can leave Alcatraz here and pick him up after.*

He replied with a thumbs-up emoji and a message. *Had a great sleep last night. Looking forward to the massage.*

Not wanting the girls to get any ideas about her and Rob, she didn't tell them or anyone else. This was an experiment to test their attitudes when they were both calm and relaxed and spent time together, nothing more. If it helped, good. If not ... Then they'd try something else.

Wednesday morning, Alicia and Frankie, who were about the same age, arrived full of chatter and enthusiasm. Soon after, Rob pulled into the driveway. "Thanks, both of you for helping me out," Jenny said. "If I'm not back when you're ready to go, leave me a note and let me know how it went today."

She headed outside to meet him. It was a clear but

chilly autumn morning. Rob had the passenger door open and the heat on. She slid into the car. "Wow, it's cold out here. Goodbye, warmish fall days. I'm so excited about this."

On the drive, they chit-chatted about nothing in particular and got along reasonably well, reminding her how it used to be. A real pleasure. "Maddie's test is today," she reminded him.

"Damn, it slipped my mind. Should've thought to text her and wish her good luck."

"Don't worry about that—she can't use her phone until we get the test result."

"Right. Can I ask you something?" he said, his gaze flicking toward her before he turned his focus back to the road.

Crossing her fingers it wasn't about Shawn or any of her other hot button issues, she nodded. "Go ahead."

"Do you really think this massage thing will help?"

"I'm not sure, but it can't hurt to try. Why, are you nervous?"

"More like wary. I might not like it."

At least he was game enough to see it through. She admired him for that. Such a good guy. She smiled to herself. "I'm pretty sure you will. Thanks for agreeing to it."

They reached the park, then pulled into the entrance. "It's not too busy yet—lots of slots available," she noted as he drove toward the resort and pulled into a space.

"I checked a map last night. The spa is on the lower level of the resort, not far from here. Let's walk."

She was impressed he'd bothered to look it up. They grabbed their things and headed toward the resort. "I haven't been to this park in ages," she said.

"The leaves are turning and look so pretty." Memories flooded her, of coming here with Rob to talk, walk around, and be together, away from her parents and his.

"It's been over a year for me. I'll definitely come back and do some trail hiking and maybe a run with a couple of guys."

"That'll be fun. Do you remember the first time we came here together?"

He nodded. "It was early summer, and Bobby Mills had gotten his driver's license. He was sixteen, a year ahead of us, and we envied him. You were friends with his girlfriend, Pris, and she got him to pick us up. We had a picnic near the lake. Then we took a walk in the woods. They went one way, we went another."

"That's when you kissed me." Jenny could almost feel the tingle in her lips and the way her heart had soared. "My first real kiss, and wow."

"I was blown away, too," he said. "I was so hot for you."

"Seemed forever before you finally kissed me. I was skeptical and impatient." He'd picked a beautiful place to do it—under the lofty, centuries-old ash tree that stood about six yards from the lake. Folklore claimed that kissing there would lead to finding true and lasting love. Which, of course, hadn't worked for her and Rob.

"I was nervous. Until it happened, I wasn't sure you'd let me."

"I only sent you a billion signals."

"Back then, I was pretty clueless about stuff like that."

"I get that now. Maturity-wise, boys are a good three years behind girls, and they stay that way for a long time."

"Seems about right. What can I say but mea culpa way back then."

He chuckled at his corny reply, and for some reason more than nostalgia washed over her. Try turned on. Over her ex? Big no-no. *Stop it,* she cautioned. "Let's go in."

WITH NO IDEA what to expect, Rob entered the spa with Jenny. The check-in desk was clean and neat. Soft, wordless music floated in the air, creating a soothing ambiance. That and the attractive woman about his age behind the desk made for a friendly set-up for spa customers.

"Hi. I'm Ella," she said with a smile. Her eyes widened as she recognized him. "I know you—you're Rob, Mr. October. I have the calendar. Wait'll I tell my friends!"

Used to the excited reaction, he flashed a perfunctory smile of his own. He wasn't interested in flirting. To his relief, she didn't seem to be, either. "Thanks for supporting the Guff's Lake Fire Department." He nodded for Jenny to take over the conversation.

Her smile was as muted as his. "We're here for our full-body massages—Jenny Carver and you already know Rob Carver."

Ella tapped something on her screen. "I have you down for a couple's massage."

Jenny frowned. "What? No—"

"What's a couple's massage?" Rob asked at the same time.

"Your massages are in the same room. It's a lovely experience."

"But we're not a couple," Jenny said.

"Divorced for years," he added.

"Oh." Ella tapped again on her screen. "I'm afraid we only have the one space available this morning."

"But I really need this massage now," Jenny wheedled, reminding Rob of Maddie and Britt when they wanted something badly.

"I'm sorry about the mistake. I'm happy to rebook you separately for another time."

Jenny bit her lip. "I'm not super comfortable about this couple's thing. What do you think, Rob?"

"It's tastefully done," Ella assured her. "You each have your own therapist, and you're shielded from each other by a privacy curtain."

Rob didn't have any concerns. He liked the idea, and since he and Jenny were getting along so well ... "I'm sure we'll manage just fine."

"All right, we'll do it."

"Excellent." Ella beamed at them. "The men's and women's changing rooms are down the hall. There are lockers to store your belongings and robes and slippers for you."

"Do we wear anything under our robes?" he asked.

"No, unless you're uneasy otherwise. Our massage therapists are professional and discreet and won't make you feel uncomfortable. Should that happen, speak up right away. Any other questions?"

"None for me," Jenny said.

Figuring he'd find out what he needed to know along the way, Rob shook his head.

After you change, please sit in the waiting room. Your therapists will come and get you. While you wait, help yourselves to water and the snacks on the table."

Minutes later, Rob exited the changing room in nothing but a dark gray robe and slippers. Jenny soon followed in a white robe. He guessed she was also naked underneath. Red-blooded male that he was, he got turned on. *Nope*, he ordered and dispatched the thought. He took a seat in the waiting room and picked up a magazine to browse.

Jenny swallowed. "Now I'm nervous."

"Why? You've done this before. You said you really liked it."

"Yes, but I wasn't in the same room with my ex."

"Don't worry, I won't get any ideas." None he intended to act on.

Her eyes narrowed slightly in warning. "Make sure you don't."

Moments later, two women appeared. One was short, solid, and young, the other taller and a good ten years her senior. "I'm Tabitha," the older woman said. "I'm here for you, Rob."

"And I'm Arjuna, Jenny. Please follow us."

Massage by a female? Suddenly, Rob was nervous, too.

9

After Jenny slipped out of her robe and pulled a lightweight blanket over herself, she told Arjuna the areas of her body that needed particular attention. After taking a few deep, calming breaths, the masseuse directed her to lie on her stomach. The comfortable headrest included an open center for her face. She assumed Rob was in a similar position, but thanks to the privacy curtain, she had no idea. Perfect. Shortly after Arjuna began to work her magic, she relaxed with a sigh and closed her eyes. "That feels so good."

She heard Rob tell Tabitha he was sore from work. Like Ella, she recognized him. "You're on this year's firefighters calendar, aren't you? You're a true hero."

"I do my best. It's rewarding work but hard on my body."

"I can feel the tightness in your back. Do you want me to be gentle or firm?"

"Firm."

Then all conversation stopped. Despite the privacy curtain, the hypnotic massage, and her closed eyes, Jenny never forgot Rob was in the room. Some four or five feet separated them, and his sounds were easy to decipher. A groan now and then, followed by Tabitha asking if she should ease up. "No," he said. "It hurts so good."

Jenny did a little sighing herself as Arjuna tackled the kinks in her neck and back. The hour went by quickly, and when the massage ended, she felt wonderful. "Thank you for this," she told Arjuna.

"You're welcome. I hope to see you again soon. I'll leave you to slip into your robe and go back to the changing room."

When both massage therapists left, Jenny sat up and put her robe on. "Did time pass as quickly for you as it did me?" she asked through the curtain.

"Way too fast. I wouldn't have minded staying longer."

"I know what you mean. I'll meet you where we checked in."

"See you there."

In the dressing room, she put on her clothes. Her skin felt soft, and she was as refreshed as if she'd awakened from a long, restful nap. Not a bit of tension. She felt incredibly sensual and sexy, and she knew why. Her inner woman wanted to come out and play. With Rob. She wanted him.

Talk about misguided and dangerous. Going there would only tangle up their relationship more than it already was. Good thing he'd never know. Stifling her feelings, she headed into the check-in area. He was standing at the desk, his big, gorgeous self in a relaxed, self-assured pose that was irresistible. It was all she could do not to run her hands down his hard chest.

What in the world had gotten into her?

She swallowed hard and made sure to stand out of

touching distance. "How much do I owe you?" she asked, focusing on the woman behind the desk. It wasn't Ella. She must've gone to lunch.

"Your husband already paid."

"But he isn't my—never mind." No point in correcting the woman when she probably wouldn't see her again.

"Did you like it?" she asked Rob as they headed up a flight of stairs.

"Very much. I feel great." A genuine smile lit up his face, the kind he used only with the people he was close to—pearly whites showing, eyes crinkling at the corners. "Thanks for suggesting this and setting it up. Suddenly, I'm super hungry. Care to test ourselves over lunch?"

He wasn't the only one hungry, although he meant his stomach. "Let's. You paid for the massages, I'll treat for lunch."

"Okay. We'll eat, then I'll take you home."

"Before the bus drops the twins off," she said. "I don't want them knowing anything about this and getting ideas." She had enough of those of her own, which she intended to ignore. At least Rob wasn't giving her any steamy looks. It helped take the edge off her shocking longing.

No sooner than the thought formed than her devilish inner woman went rogue. Like a woman in a shampoo commercial, she gave her head a sexy shake and fluffed her hair. "Do I look as relaxed as I feel?" To her own ears, she didn't sound at all like herself.

He glanced at her with curiosity and something more. "You definitely seem different."

"I *feel* different," she admitted. Not wanting to say or do something she'd regret, she turned the subject to lunch. "I'm thinking we should eat at the Coffee

Shack. It's close-by and shouldn't be too busy at this hour. It's a gorgeous, clear day, and the view of the lake and the Siskiyous should be fabulous."

The casual restaurant was a longtime favorite and popular with both locals and tourists. "I haven't been there in years," Rob said.

"Neither have I. Should we try it?"

"You had me at 'Shack.'"

STILL FEELING great after the massage, Rob smiled at Jenny from across their table at the Shack. "What a great idea for lunch. Like you said, we're late enough after the lunch crowd to score a great place to sit, right in front of a window and enjoy the view while we eat."

"We lucked out, for sure." She smiled back.

Look at them, getting along so well. Sharing the massage room seemed to have bonded them, a nice change from the usual tension they felt around each other. Now if he could corral his wayward lust, everything would be fine. The massage had unlocked a long-buried desire he hadn't realized he'd held on to.

"What's on your agenda this afternoon?" he asked while they enjoyed fruit cobbler for dessert.

"Thanks to Alicia and Frankie, I have the rest of the day to myself—depending, of course, on the twins." She checked her watch. "In about an hour, Maddie will take her test. If she feels good about it, it'll be a nice afternoon for all of us. Let's hope she aces it."

Lost in watching her expressive face, Rob barely heard a word she said. The curve of her lips, the sparkle in her eyes—she was radiant in a way he hadn't seen in a long time. Captivating.

"What are you looking at?" she said, wearing a slight frown. "Do I have something on my face?"

He shook his head, fighting his growing desire. "Promise you won't get upset."

"When we're getting along so well? It's the furthest thing from my mind. Tell me. It'll be another test of how well we do together when we're relaxed."

Their gazes locked and telegraphed things better left unsaid. "Let's get out of here and drive to a place where we can be outside and enjoy the view without windows. I'll tell you then." He signaled for the check.

Jenny paid the bill, and they left. A short drive later, they reached the observation point he wanted to show her, a secluded spot surrounded by Douglas Firs and oak and maple trees in eye-popping golds and reds. "Have you been here?" he asked as they exited the car.

"No, and I can't believe I've missed it all these years. What a treat."

After a few minutes of admiring the sparkling lake and majestic mountains, she turned to him. "I need to get home soon, so tell me now about this thing that might make me mad."

"All right. You look incredibly hot. Does that offend you?"

"Not in the least because I happen to feel the same about you."

"No way." Relieved at this unexpected piece of good luck. He stepped in closer and pulled her into his arms. Sucking in a breath, he waited for her to push him away. She didn't, instead stared up at him, her big eyes filled with emotion he couldn't decipher. "Your mouth—I have to taste you," he said. "If you don't want that, stop me now. Otherwise—"

She rose up and silenced him with a kiss of her own.

He ignited like a parched tree helpless against a fire. Their lips fused and opened to make way for their tongues. He inched back. "You taste as good as I remember. Better, I think. Let me make sure."

Burning for her, he kissed her again, several times. Stopping wasn't easy, but necessary. "Better than ever."

"I think so, too." She stroked his cheek with her soft fingers.

They were both breathing hard. "I want you," he said.

"Me, too, from the time you picked me up. But that's crazy. I don't think we should be doing this."

He agreed, although his hunger made it hard to step back. "I'll take you home now."

It was a mostly silent ride until they were a short distance from her place. "I guess the massage idea was a good one," she said. "I doubt we need any other therapy."

"Let's sleep on it and see what happens." Although he had a hunch that tonight, sleeping wouldn't be easy.

Breaking to a stop in the driveway, he brushed the hair behind her ears and swore she had stars in her eyes. So beautiful. He fought not to kiss her again. "I'll be in touch."

"Okay. Thanks for treating me to the massage. We should do this again."

"Get a couple's massage or mess around?" he teased.

She started to say something, but the rumble of the school bus pulling to a stop cut her off. "Oh, no, the bus is here! Let's get out of the car." They exited and she added, "Quick, what are we going to tell them?"

He had no problem coming up with an answer. "That we don't want to fight anymore and got together to talk about it. It's the truth."

"Except for the parts we left out." She blushed. "They should buy that, right?"

The girls were almost at the car. "We're about to find out."

10

Worried about what the twins might think, Jenny put on a calm face. "How was school, Britt? How do you think you did on the test, Maddie?"

"I won't know till Mrs. Williams hands it back," Maddie said. "You went somewhere with Dad." She glanced from Jenny to Rob.

"You didn't mention that this morning," Britt chimed in, shooting them a quizzical look.

"I, um—" Jenny stumbled.

"I was coming here anyway, to pick up Alcatraz," Rob filled in. "Getting together was a spur-of-the-moment thing, so I left him here. We're both tired of being so uncomfortable around each other and decided to talk and make some changes."

Both girls squinted at them, and Jenny wondered what they were thinking. Better set them straight. "Don't go jumping to conclusions. As your father said, we're serious about changing our ways. Something we should've done a long time ago. Our failure to get along better isn't fair to you girls, your dad's crewmates, or anyone else." The dog was barking up a storm, no doubt having heard their voices. "Alcatraz is eager to see you girls and your father. I'll go get him."

"Good boy," she crooned as the dog's tail wagged furiously. "Let's go see Rob and the twins." She leashed him and returned to the front yard.

More tail wagging and a few licks and joyous yips before Rob ended the visit. "Thanks for taking care of him, Jenny, and for talking earlier. Let me know about that test, Maddie. As soon as you're off restriction, text me. And Britt, I want to know how you did on that essay you worked so hard on over the weekend. You two have a good rest of the week."

As soon as he left, Jenny started toward the front door. "It's cold out here. Let's go inside."

After the chill in the air, the warmth in the house felt good. Alicia had left a note that she and Frankie had enjoyed the day, and all was well.

The twins dropped their backpacks and jackets on the living room sofa, then headed toward the kitchen for something to eat.

"Tell me about your days," Jenny said while they sat at the kitchen table and attacked their cheese and crackers and glugged colas as if they hadn't eaten or drunk anything in days.

"It was fine," Maddie said. Britt nodded.

Which was all they ever said, but she always asked anyway. "Halloween is a week from Friday. Are you going out trick-or-treating?"

Maddie huffed as if the question irritated her. "As if, Mom, We're too old. We're going to Lainey Wycliff's for a party. There's a sleepover after for girls only. But the party is for boys, too. I'm meeting Hudson there."

"Theo will be there, too."

Jenny had briefly met both boys a few weeks earlier, when she'd picked the girls up for dentist appointments. They seemed nice enough. "Sounds fun."

"Lainey's really Maddie's friend," Britt said, "so I won't be sleeping over."

"No problem—you'll be sleeping at your dad's that weekend, and I know he'll want to pick you up. We can talk more about that later. I need to check my email, so clean up your mess when you finish—"

"What's really going on with you and Dad?" Britt interrupted.

Jenny didn't have an answer for that—she had no idea what might happen between her and Rob. Nothing close to getting back together, but with the attraction pulsing between them ... Regardless of what did or didn't happen, she wouldn't be sharing any of it with her daughters. "We already explained that we're figuring out how to get along better. We've been way too tense around each other, and we want things to be different. Changing our ways could take a while."

Maddie and Britt shared a look. This time, Maddie spoke. "I'll bet Shawn doesn't like that at all."

Jenny hadn't told them about the decision to part ways. "It's really not his business. We're not seeing each other anymore."

Both girls wide-eyed her. "When did you decide that?" Maddie asked.

"The night we ran into you and your father at Harvey's."

Maddie threw her a dirty look. "That was almost a week ago. You expect us to tell you everything, but you never tell us anything. Neither does Dad!"

Jenny's mother had also kept things from her and had infuriated her the same as Maddie. It wasn't until she'd grown up that she understood—kids didn't need to know everything. Keeping certain things out of their radar was a way to protect them. Still, she should've said something sooner. "I didn't mention it because it wasn't a big deal, and I figured you wouldn't care."

"We do care!" Like Maddie, Britt was outraged. "When you have a boyfriend, we deserve to know when things get serious or when you breakup."

She sounded like a little general giving a no-nonsense order. Jenny had a hunch that at times, she sounded that way, too. "Shawn never mattered that much, and I wasn't sad when it happened. We didn't have a fight or anything. It was a mutual decision."

"You still should've told us. We're not little kids, Mom. We don't want you keeping things from us."

Britt had a valid point. "Got it," Jenny said, knowing she'd limit any information to what made sense.

"Good," Maddie said. "Britt and I never liked Shawn."

"Did you break up because we were so rude that night?" Britt asked, biting her lip as if she felt guilty for her behavior.

"You embarrassed me, yes, but that's not the reason we broke up. I didn't like him that much."

"You like Dad, though."

"He's your father, so of course, I do. The positive thing that came from that night is that we've been getting along pretty well now, and we mean to stay that way. That's all there is to it."

Neither daughter said a word, and their expressions suddenly blanked. They likely doubted she and Rob would ever relax around each other like normal people, or maybe their hopes were pinned on a total reconciliation between them. Neither was true, but she wasn't sure how to convince them. Rob might have an idea about that. "I may as well start dinner," she said.

"It's too early to eat," Britt pointed out. "I'm going upstairs and starting on my homework."

"I'll come with you." Maddie took her plate to the sink.

"Don't leave it there," Jenny reminded her. Grumbling, she loaded it into the dishwasher. "I'll call you when it's time to eat."

The twins headed up the stairs, speaking in voices too low for her ears. She imagined they were talking about her and Rob.

She couldn't do a thing about that except pretend nothing major had changed between them except their momentous decision to get along. That much was true—if she didn't count the high-voltage attraction still sizzling inside her.

~

IN NO MOOD TO start her homework, Maddie left her assignments in her backpack. Britt did the same. There was too much to talk about. "I can't believe Mom and Dad went out together today."

"I know," her sister agreed. "Wouldn't it be amaze-balls if they really did get along from now on?"

Maddie wasn't sure. "I don't see that happening, but I swear I saw Dad touch Mom's cheek in the car. That was before they noticed us."

Britt frowned. "Why would he do that?"

"Duh. Because he likes her?"

"No way!" Britt said, way too loud and gleeful.

Wary their mom might be eavesdropping, Maddie put her finger over her lips. "Talk softer."

"Sorry," Britt replied in a much quieter voice.

"Maybe they'll get along so well, they'll get back together. We were too young to remember what it was like when they were happy, but what if it happened again?" She laid her hands together over her heart. "Wouldn't that be great?"

Maddie was all for it but knew better. "Don't count on that. You know how they're friendly sometimes and the next minute super uncomfortable with each other again? Getting along right now is probably one of those times."

"All I know is, I have hope." Britt leaned in. "Did I hear right about you and Hudson during lunch?"

Maddie had no idea what she meant. "What did you hear?"

"That you guys came back from lunch break looking different."

Different? "Who said that?"

"I'm not sure—I heard it from someone who heard it from someone."

Maddie snorted. "We looked different, how?"

"Like you had sex."

Confused, Maddie frowned. "What does that look like?"

"How should I know? Did you or not?"

Maddie rolled her eyes. "If we had, I'd have told you. We couldn't mess around like we usually do today because it's getting too cold outside. The weather turned so fast." She lowered her voice to barely above a whisper. "We made a decision to do it Halloween night. I guess we looked different because we're excited about it."

Britt's jaw dropped. "But you'll be at Lainey's party. So will I, Theo, and a bunch of other kids. And don't forget their parents. Only one of them is taking the younger kids out trick-or-treating. The other one will chaperone us."

"Duh. I'm sleeping over, remember? I'm going to sneak out and meet Hudson late that night, when Lainey's parents will be asleep."

Britt worked her lip between her teeth, all worried. "I hope you don't get caught."

"Don't worry, we won't."

"It's even colder at night than it is during the day so you can't be outdoors. Where will you go?"

"Hudson's brother Beau said we could use his van. His girlfriend lives around the corner from Lainey, and he'll park it along a side street a few blocks from there. It has a mattress in the back and everything. We're going to meet there at midnight." Britt was silent and chewing her lip again. "Don't worry," Maddie reassured her. "I'm not. It's going to be special."

Her twin nodded and opened her backpack. "I'm going to do my homework now."

With no phone privileges yet—please, please, please let the test results be good enough to satisfy her parents—Maddie did the same. By the time their mom called them to dinner, she was halfway through it.

fter missing the poker game the previous week, Rob arrived at Rafe's place—this was his turn to host—stoked for a fun evening with whoever showed up to play. Thanks to shrewd investments in real estate, Rafe and his wife Jillian lived in style. Big, comfy home with a view of the Siskiyous and Guff's Lake. Having married the previous month, they were newlyweds and very happy.

Besides Rafe and him, four other guys showed up —Daniel, Liam, Nate, and Ethan. Good people to hang with, but then, Rob felt that way about all his crewmates. Competition was fierce in a friendly way, with cigars, beer or pop, and junk food for all. Rob brought chips and dip, and the rest of the guys brought other snacks. They also talked smack about anything and everything and traded raunchy barbs. Which all-in-all made for a great time.

Each player tossed $2.00 in the kitty. Winner take all, and Rob aimed to leave with the winnings, a whopping ten bucks richer.

"Do any of you want to help out at the Halloween party?" Nate asked at one point. The firehouse sponsored multiple events for the community throughout the year. "This year is our crew's turn to host. It's next Friday night, and we need volunteers. Captain Comings and Adam will be there for sure, and their wives and kids will stop by. We're expecting the usual crowd of Guff's Lake families. Becca and I signed up to help." She was Nate's girlfriend.

Rob spoke right up. "I'll do it." That was his weekend to have the twins, but they'd be at their own party that night, along with their boyfriends and other kids their age. At the end of that party, Maddie and several of her girlfriends planned to sleep over there —provided she did well on her test. The festivities at the station ended at eight-thirty p.m., giving him plenty of time to pick up Britt. He'd come back for Maddie the following morning.

The game was winding down and he was doing pretty well and having fun when Rafe eyeballed him. "How are things with you and Jenny?"

Huh? Rob scratched the back of his neck. "Why are you asking?"

"I'm curious."

So much for keeping his personal life private. "You've probably heard about Harvey's. That was a bad night, way too tense. We talked and decided to—" Not about to mention couple's massage, which would cause a lot of noise and questions, he said, "We're working on other solutions."

"Such as?" Daniel asked. Rob shrugged, and the guy went on. "When I picked up Toad after our shift this week, Jenny wasn't there. Alicia and Frankie said she'd gone somewhere with you."

"Is that so." Rafe eyed him as in *spill*.

He could be relentless, and this was one of those times. Jenny wouldn't like Rob saying anything, but the dude had backed him into a corner. "Now don't jump to conclusions, okay? We decided to get massages and find out if being truly relaxed was any help with the tension."

"Where did you get the massages?" Rafe asked.

"Guff's Lake Resort."

"Jillian and I did a couple's massage there once. We each had a masseuse. It was nice and kinda hot even though we couldn't see each other. We were separated but felt connected because we were doing it together, and we both really enjoyed it. Did you get yours at the same time?" Rob nodded. "Two singles, huh?"

"Couples, but only because the scheduler mistakenly booked us that way and there was nothing else available." He swallowed, remembering. His buddies scrutinized him and he shrugged. "Like you said, Rafe, we each had our own massage therapist and plenty of privacy. So don't go getting any ideas."

Although he sure had. He kept thinking about those kisses and the unexpected awakening of his dormant desire, but he had no intention of letting it loose again. No sense complicating things by stirring up more trouble. Best to keep his distance from her unless it involved the girls or Alcatraz.

"The look on your face gives me plenty of ideas," Liam said. "I'm thinking things got hot."

"In a massage room?" Rob made a *pfft* sound. Snickers of disbelief followed. "I mean it," he said. Good thing he wasn't Pinocchio or his nose would be a foot long. "We left completely relaxed and decided to have lunch as a test and see how that went."

"Did it work?"

More than he'd wanted to, and at the same time not nearly enough. "Really well. We didn't get all tense with each other. We done here?"

"Not quite. How do you plan to maintain that? You can't get massages every time you see each other."

"No, but we proved we can relax around each other, a real plus. There's hope. Is that a satisfactory answer for you?"

"More or less." Rafe checked his watch. "Jillian will be home soon. Let's clean up this mess."

In the end, Daniel won the kitty. "Crap," Rob said, putting his stogie out in an ashtray. "I'll get you next time."

As SOON AS the girls caught the bus to school Friday morning, Jenny phoned Rob to let him know about Maddie. A simple information call, the kind they shared where their daughters were concerned.

"Hey," he answered.

Over the years she'd known him, she'd grown used to hearing his deep voice. This time though, it thrummed through her as it hadn't in years and made her weak with longing. Which was insane, given the tension between them. Right now, it was almost nonexistent, but she wouldn't be surprised if it crept back. She half-wished she'd never kissed him after the massages. Never mind, it wouldn't happen again.

"Jenny? You there?"

She cleared her throat and pulled herself together. "I am. I hope I'm not bothering you."

"I'm on my way to Mayor Blinkins to make her car look its best."

"Wow, you travel in high circles. I won't keep you long. I have good news—Maddie got a B-plus on her test! I told her, 'look what you can do when you're motivated!'"

"That's fantastic, both the grade and your positivity. When did you find out?"

Complimenting her positivity as if she'd done something she rarely did? Calling on what she learned in therapy, she pulled in a calming breath. "I'm positive lots of the time," she reminded him in her most reasonable tone. "I found out yesterday. She was supposed to call and tell you, but she got busy on her phone and social media and all the stuff she missed while she was on restriction. It's been nice talking to her without the devices. I'm going to miss that."

"I meant the positive comment as a compliment, Jenny. Say 'thank you, Rob.'"

Jeesh. "Thanks, Rob."

"You're welcome. FYI, I know you're mostly positive."

She'd overreacted, she realized, and silently chastised herself for being so darn sensitive to the things he said. "I keep meaning to tell you that both girls cornered me the other day and demanded I stop hiding things from them and start talking about what's going on with me date-wise, including when the dating starts and when it ends."

"Really. Where did that come from?"

"They were upset I didn't tell them right away about calling it quits with Shawn. Anyway, they reminded me that they're not little kids anymore and deserve to know."

"They have a point."

"And I agreed to be more open—about some things. There are certain parts of my life I don't even share with my closest friends."

"You and me both." He let out a low, sexy laugh that, like his voice, stirred unwanted heat through her. "I'll text Maddie and tell her I'm proud of her and knew she could do it. Look how well we just handled ourselves."

"We're earned our own B-plus." She smiled. "Maddie will appreciate that text." He was such a good dad and also a good man. "If you don't hear back from her, it's likely because she's busy with Halloween plans. Lately, all she and Britt talk about is the party they're invited to. Decorations, costumes, who's going … You'd think they were invited to a star-studded event."

"Kids and their parties. Good thing it falls on a Friday night. They can sleep in the next day. Speaking of Halloween, I volunteered to help out at the fire-house party. That's my weekend to have the girls, but their plans free me up."

"Nice of you to do that. It's bound to be busy. If you're short-handed, I'm happy to help out." Had she really offered to lend a hand? At least with a big crowd there, she wouldn't get distracted by the man she ought to steer clear of. "Most of the kids in the neigh-borhood go to the mall or fire department for their trick-or-treating, so I won't have anything else to do. Just in case, I'll set out a bowl of candy with a sign for kids to help themselves. Visiting the firehouse after such a long time will be fun." She meant that, then paused. "Do you think people will talk about us?"

"I'm sure they will. I played poker the other night, and the guys all knew about the fiasco at Harvey's. I told them we're working on getting along better. They know about the couple's massage."

Jenny groaned. "I hope Maddie and Britt don't find out. Since the afternoon they saw us in your car, they're very enthusiastic about us trying to get along. We don't want them thinking we might get back to-gether because we won't," she stated firmly for both her and Rob's benefit. In case he had other ideas. "It'd be a disaster in the making." She shuddered at the thought. "Which is why they shouldn't know anything about the two of us. But I *will* tell them I'm helping out at the firehouse party."

"They'll like that. I'm with you on the rest. Blame what happened with us the other day on the massages and the mood they put us both in."

So he was over it now. Jenny told herself she was relieved, but her good mood dimmed some. That bothered and confused her. She didn't want to start anything with Rob that remotely resembled a romantic relationship. The problem was, certain body parts had other ideas. Forget that. Unwanted lust would lead to big trouble. She needed to meet a hot new man and forget about Rob.

"I'm almost at the Mayor's office, so I'd best go," he said. "As always, I'll see you Sunday when I drop off Alcatraz."

12

S aturday morning, Jenny heard from her father. "Hi, Dad," she said. "It's been a while, and I'm glad you called. How are you?"

"Busy." As the founder of Baldwin Audio, an audio book and media company he'd built into a very profitable business, he always was. "And no, we're not switching to AI. I refuse to do that, and my clients and narrators are pleased."

She smiled at his slightly offended tone. "I know that, Dad, and if I ever run into anyone who asks, I'll be sure to tell them. Hey, would you like to have dinner tonight? The girls have plans of their own, but I don't have any." Now that Maddie was off restriction, she'd made a date to hang out with Lainey, her bestie, and some of her other friends to work on the Halloween party Lainey was hosting. Britt was seeing a movie with her own friends.

Jenny wanted to update her father about Maddie and the test. Unless he'd heard something. In Guff's Lake, you never knew who spread what. Like everyone else, he enjoyed gossip. Was that the reason for his call? Or had he found out about her argument with Rob at Harvey's? Even the thought made her cringe.

Before she could fish around and find out what he knew without actually telling him, he went on.

"I'm sorry to miss them. I called to invite all of you to dinner at my house, but we'll manage without them. Adelle and I like to cook together, and this is a good time for you to meet her."

He'd waited three years after Jenny's mom had passed away before he'd started dating. Several tries and failures later, he'd met Adelle. They'd been seeing each other for a good six months, but he'd never offered to introduce her. That he wanted them to meet meant he must really like her, which was good news. "That sounds great. What should I bring?"

"Just yourself. We're making chicken alfredo, homemade bread, and a grilled vegetable salad."

"My mouth is already watering. When did you turn into a gourmet chef?"

"Adelle's been teaching me. As it turns out, I like to cook."

"What fun. I don't want to come empty-handed. Why don't I bring a bottle of wine and something from Carleton's Bakery? I stopped there recently, and their cupcakes and cookies are out of this world."

"Okay. See you at six."

Later, leaving the twins, who promised to be home by ten o'clock, Jenny arrived on time at her dad's. A year or so after becoming a widower, he'd sold the home where she'd grown up and downsized to a smaller place in an equally upscale neighborhood. He answered the door in a food-stained apron, greeted her with a hug, and then gestured to the attractive woman standing beside him. Silver streaks mingled with her thick, chin-length, dark hair. "This is Adelle. Meet my daughter, Jenny."

The woman's smile was warm and her gaze bright

and interested. "I finally get to meet the apple of your dad's eye."

Jenny liked her immediately. "Is that what I am? It's good to finally meet you as well. I hope you don't mind white wine. I like it with chicken. It's chilled and ready to drink. Should I put it in the fridge? I'll take the cookies into the kitchen, too."

"It's okay to open the wine. It'll go well with the appetizers."

Adelle went with her to get an assorted tray of delicious cheeses and crackers. While they nibbled, Jenny told her about her two businesses. Adelle talked about her job as the office manager at an urgent care facility.

A little while later, they headed into the dining room for dinner. The meal was a fun and tasty affair, with a good deal of laughter and lively conversation. Near the end of it, Adelle had a phone call.

"I need to answer this," she apologized. "It's Heather—my daughter. She's going through rough times and I want to be there for her. Herb will explain." She headed into another room.

"I like her, Dad," Jenny said. She loved how they interacted with each other and the lack of tension between them—the way a couple ought to be. The way he'd never been with her mom. She so wanted that with Rob.

He smiled. "I do, too. Why don't I bring her to Thanksgiving? That way, the girls can meet her."

"Sounds like a plan. What's going on with her daughter?"

The smile faded. "She's having financial difficulties due to a husband with bad habits."

"Drugs?"

He nodded. "And gambling."

That sounded like living in hell. "What a shame. I can't imagine."

"It's been rough." He didn't elaborate further and she didn't want to pry more than she already had, so she filled him in about Maddie. "Now that she's redeemed herself at school, things are good, but when I grounded her for skipping class and being on the verge of failing the course, she got really mad at me. She even asked if she could spend an extra night with Rob last weekend. Britt went, too."

"But she got over it, like you did when your mom clamped down on you."

"Yes, but I worry. I don't want her to grow up resenting me." It was the closest Jenny had come to sharing the resentment, some of which she still harbored, toward her mother.

"Surely with age and perspective, you realize your mother behaved as she did out of love for you," her dad pointed out.

"Of course, but my teen years were worse than they needed to be. I'm doing things differently and not lecturing so much or judging their boyfriends so harshly." At least, she wanted to. "That is, trying, but I usually fail. It's not easy."

Her father gave her a kindly pat on the shoulder. "No matter what, you're their mother and they love you."

"Rob said the same thing."

His face lit up. "How is Rob?"

Hot, still a good kisser, making her crazy with longing. "He's good."

"You're blushing."

"I am not!" she said, realizing she sounded as rattled as she was. She cleared her throat. "Things between us have been so tense for years, but now we're working on changing that."

"Huh." He gave her the shrewd look he wore when he heard something he didn't quite buy.

"It's the truth, Dad. I'll clear the table and bring in plates for the cookies."

Shortly after she loaded the dishwasher and laid out the dessert, Adelle returned to the dining room. The conversation focused on her daughter, who'd decided to file for divorce. Sorry for them all but glad for the shift in her father's attention, Jenny relaxed.

BY THE TIME SUNDAY DAWNED, Rob had grown way too eager to see Jenny. Despite distracting himself and focusing on other things, he ended up driving to her place earlier than usual. "Hope you don't mind," he told his collie. "I want to see the twins." The pooch made a sound similar to a disbelieving snort. "Guess I can't fool you," Rob told him.

At the door, Alcatraz let out a joyful yip.

Seconds later, Maddie opened it. "Hi, Dad. You're early tonight. Hi, Alcatraz." She gave the dog lots of love. She hadn't been in a mood this good in a long time.

"Is Britt upstairs studying?" he asked, wondering where both she and Jenny were.

Maddie shook her head. "She and mom are at the store, picking up candy for Halloween."

Then he wouldn't see Jenny. Disappointment warred with relief. Better to avoid her. "Tell her I'll pick him up Wednesday morning."

"She knows that, Dad. I went to Lainey's Friday

night with some friends to plan the Halloween party. It's gonna be so fun. Can I show you my costume?

For the last two years, she'd been blasé about the holiday. Seeing her excited was a welcome change. He gave an enthusiastic nod. "Sure."

"I'll be right back."

Seconds later, she brought two items downstairs—a black dress and a black wig. "You're going to be a witch," he guessed.

"Wrong." She rolled her eyes at him, as if he were an idiot. "I'm a vampire."

"I couldn't tell—all I see is a long dress and that wig."

"Halloween night, people will know. I'm going to have long, scarlet fingernails, this wig, and fangs."

Picturing that, he grinned. "Send me photos of that. Or wait—I'll see you in costume when I pick up Britt. I'll take photos then."

"You won't be picking me up that night. Mom told you about the sleepover, right?"

He nodded. "Text when you're up and ready the next morning, and I'll come get you."

"Britt's going as a banana." Maddie laughed. "It's so funny."

"I'll bet. Your boyfriend, uh," Rob paused, trying to recall the latest kid's name, then remembered. "Hudson will be there, right?"

"Uh-huh." Maddie wouldn't quite meet his eyes, making him wonder. "Britt's boyfriend, Theo, will be there, too."

"I'll look forward to meeting them both. While you and Britt are at your party, I'll be handing out candy at the firehouse."

"Mom mentioned that. You haven't done that for a

long time, and I don't think she ever has. Are you both wearing costumes?"

"Yeah, but I don't know yet what mine will be. Your mom hasn't mentioned hers, either. Guess I'll see both you and Britt in your costumes when I pick her up."

Maddie's phone signaled a message. She glanced at the screen. "Okay, Dad. Bye."

Not wanting to leave Alcatraz in the house without Jenny or at least one of the twins around, he waited a few minutes. In the end, tired of hanging by himself, he hollered up the stairs for Maddie to come down and keep his dog company.

As soon as she did, he headed out.

13

After Jenny dropped the girls off at the party Friday night, she headed for the firehouse to help with the trick-or-treaters. In a Rapunzel costume, complete with a cheap gold-color wig of ridiculously long hair, she felt like someone else. She walked into a happy, noisy affair, perfect for a Halloween party. A bunch of kids and parents were crowded into the lobby area, and firefighters milled around talking to people and handing out candy and stickers. Various girlfriends and wives also lent a hand.

Firefighters and their partners waved and called out greetings, which she returned as she searched for Rob. She didn't spot him until her gaze lit on a tall male wearing the grin she knew so well. He was hunkered down to chat with a little boy about seven or eight, decked out like Harry Potter. Rob wore a white lab coat and ugly fake glasses. A fuzzy gray mop of a wig obscured his dark brown fade.

As she made her way toward him, she couldn't help but laugh. "Hey there, stranger," she called out over the noise, tossing her fake, bright gold hair over her shoulder—or trying. Too much hair and too little flexibility getting the strands to move together. Should've braided the thing at home.

He chuckled. "Let me guess—Rapunzel is here. This is Harry Potter." He glanced up. "And his mom, um—I didn't catch your name."

"Jess," she said, looking pleased he'd asked. Like so many women, she had stars in her eyes.

Jenny didn't blame the woman—as long as she didn't make a play for him. The thought appalled her. What did she care? "It's nice to meet you, Jess and Harry," she said, offering a smile. "I hope you're getting lots of candy, Harry."

The beaming boy showed off his bag of treats before he and his mom moved on to another firefighter and other treats. Jenny and Rob struck up a conversation in loud voices in order to hear each other over the noise. "Who are you supposed to be?" she asked.

"Can't you tell? A mad scientist."

"You certainly look mad with that hair."

"Some wig, huh? Yours is pretty weird, too."

"Tell me about it. It came with the costume I ordered online. I dropped the twins off at the Wycliff's for the party. June was home, and Boyer was out trick-or-treating with their younger kids. We might see them here tonight."

"Cool." Rob liked the Wycliffs and always had. They were a solid couple with three nice kids. "Did you see the boyfriends?"

"Both of them."

"And?"

"I was able to chat a bit with each boy, but only for a few seconds before our darling daughters wanted me gone, so—"

"I can't hear you," he said and gestured her forward. "Come with me."

She'd been in the firehouse many times, but never in the room where he led her. A glance around and she guessed what it was for. "This must be the training room."

"How'd you guess?"

"The big table in the middle and the bright overhead lights. It's so quiet in here. Let's sit for a minute, but we probably shouldn't stay here too long, or people will start talking."

"That's for sure. They've talked more than enough about Harvey's." He grimaced. "You were saying?"

"That the girls shooed me away. As often as their boyfriends come and go, I doubt my opinion matters anyway." She thought a minute. "This is going to sound weird, but Hudson seemed a little too polite, like he wanted to impress me."

"Well, yeah. That's what boys do when they meet their girlfriend's mom."

"You didn't do that."

"At first, I did," Rob said. "Maybe you didn't notice."

"You had good manners, but you were genuine, not phony like Hudson." She didn't like the boy but couldn't quite put her finger on why. Which knowing little about him except that he played football, wasn't fair to him. If he and Maddie lasted longer than most teen relationships and Jenny got to know him better, she'd probably change her mind.

"You didn't care for Maddie's boyfriend. How about Theo?"

"Much more real, blushing and uncomfortable, like I was when I met your parents," she said.

Rob nodded. "They liked you right off, but your mom didn't like me at all."

"She never cared for any boy I was interested in."

For a moment, neither of them spoke. Jenny lost herself in memories—the endless battles with her mother about Rob and whatever else she didn't approve of. Oh, to hear those criticisms again. She missed the woman, even the battles. "I don't want the girls feeling that way about me. I'm trying to mellow out some, but it's hard."

"You're fine the way you are. You discipline them with love. It won't hurt them."

"That's not what you said when I grounded Maddie."

"It wasn't because of that. You kept harping on her when she already knew she was in the wrong. You're a great mom. Britt and Maddie know it, and so do I." He squeezed her hand, no doubt to reassure her.

The physical contact did more than that, triggering her feelings and the dangerous attraction to him. She glanced down at his big fingers around hers and told herself to pull out of his grasp. "We should rejoin everyone," she said, and tucked her hand safely in a skirt pocket of her costume.

"We will. But first, we should talk about what happened the other day."

She knew exactly what he meant, wanted to trace her finger over his lips for the simple pleasure of physical contact. "The kisses."

"And everything else." He caressed the knuckles of her free hand with his thumb. "I felt things I didn't want to feel. I still do, only stronger tonight. I think you're in the same boat."

Was she that easy to read? She reclaimed that hand, too. "We can't give in to this ..." At a loss for words, she paused to think. What was the name for it? "This crazy longing."

"You have no idea how many times I've reminded

myself that we have no business starting anything. It's not working. We both assumed the other day was a fluke brought on by the massages, but in the three days since then, nothing has changed for me. Maybe if we kiss again and find out if we feel any different now, it'll help us return to sanity."

Every part of her wanted that, but she was scared of what might happen then. "That's some line," she said in an effort to push the thought away. "The answer is no, thanks. It's time we went back to the lobby." The chair scraped back as she pushed to her feet. "Otherwise, they'll be gossiping about us."

Rob stood, too. "They'll gossip no matter what. We may as well give them something to talk about."

His eyes were intent on hers, too hot to look away from. Her common sense went AWOL. She stepped in closer, twined her arms around his neck, and gave in.

JENNY WAS sweet in his arms, her lips as warm and seductive as always. "God above, you taste good," he murmured.

"Be quiet and kiss me again." She tugged his head down and he caught fire. He cupped her soft rear end, pulling her against his hard-on.

She wriggled closer still. He wanted to stroke his hands up her legs but her costume was so long and bulky, he couldn't handle it. "What's with this dress? It's like a chastity belt."

She chuckled, and the mood was broken. They stepped apart. She smoothed the fabric, and he tugged his lab coat down. "I couldn't survive in clothes like these," she said. "Next year, I'll figure out something better. Ready to rejoin the crowd?"

"Better straighten that wig first."

"You should see your face. Is that a grimace?"

"The opposite. It's making me laugh."

She fished through her purse for her phone and turned the lens to selfie. "I look like a clown!" She laughed right along with him.

"I think it's cute."

"Oh, yeah? Your wig isn't any better."

He got out his phone and studied himself. "You're right. I dread the day I'll be a geezer like this." They stood side by side, joking with each other. Damn, he enjoyed laughing together. He snapped a few selfies of the two of them. "Some pair we are."

"Pair? I'm not sure *what* we are."

"We're hot for each other, that's what. Boiling hot."

"I don't want this for us, Rob. It's ... What am I trying to say?"

"I think the word you're looking for is dangerous."

"That's it. It won't happen again, will it?" she said, sounding as uncertain as he felt. "We shouldn't get tangled up that way. We can't."

"I'm with you. It'd be a mistake we'd both regret. Trouble is, I don't know if we can resist each other."

"With our daughters nearby, that shouldn't be difficult."

Rob had the uncomfortable feeling the problem wasn't going away so easily. "At least we know now the massages didn't have much to do with what happened after."

"They lowered our inhibitions, at least mine. I felt so sensuous." Jenny groaned. "Tonight is more potent."

"Definitely. Let's make a pact it won't happen again."

She nodded. "Pinky swear." He held out his little finger and she linked hers with him.

"Time to vámonos," he said.

"Not together, okay? I'll go first, then you come in."

He watched her leave, waited five minutes, and then returned to where they'd started.

14

When the firehouse festivities ended a few hours later, Rob helped clean up. Jenny stuck around and also pitched in. If anyone had seen them leave the lobby together earlier, they didn't mention it. A relief, and he and Jenny parted ways with a casual goodnight to each other.

It was almost time to pick up Britt. Now that he was away from Jenny and the noise at the firehouse, he could think clearly. He felt good about their agreement not to repeat what had happened tonight and was determined to keep a healthy physical distance from her. Even as he assured himself of that, he wanted her. Snuggled close in his bed, her head on his chest.

Clamping his jaw, he forced his hunger and the self-imposed forbidden fantasy away. When he arrived at the Wycliffs, the party was on its last legs. Many of the kids had left, but Hudson and Theo were still there. Hudson had his arm around Maddie, and when he spotted Rob, he quickly dropped it. Maddie introduced them. The kid seemed nice enough, but Rob hadn't liked that arm around her. Or the kid's ultra-politeness. Jenny had been right about that. Theo, on the other hand, didn't seem as nervous as she'd described, likely due to the evening blunting any nerves.

He took several photos of the girls together and then with the boys, all of them happy to oblige. "Remember to text me in the morning, Maddie, and I'll come get you."

"I will."

He thanked June and Boyer and left with Britt. "Did you have a good time?" he asked on the drive home.

"It was fun."

"Theo seems nice."

"He is. I like him, Dad."

"He seems to like you, too."

"I know."

Britt wore the goofy smile people got when they had strong feelings about each other. He didn't worry too much—she was too young to get serious and likely to go through a number of other boyfriends along the way.

"How was the party at the firehouse?"

"Noisy and fun." Also way too hot for his own good. "Overall, a great time. Your mom and I thought Mr. Wycliff was bringing the younger kids by, but they didn't show."

"Mom said she was going to help out there."

"I'm glad she did. We were swamped." Rob ignored his daughter's speculative expression. "Did she show you the wig that came with the Rapunzel costume?"

Britt nodded. "So gross."

"I had a mad scientist wig that was pretty bad, too," he said. "If you're wondering, we got along pretty well. I took photos of us in our costumes. I'll show you later."

"So you really are getting along."

"Yeah, and we're both relieved about that."

At home, Rob shared the photos, and Britt reciprocated. Then she headed upstairs. After watching a sitcom, he turned in. He was in a deep sleep when the phone woke him. Maddie, the screen said. Calling at twelve forty-five a.m.? Uh-oh. He jerked up and answered. "What's wrong?"

"Please come get me, Dad," she said, sobbing as she hadn't in years.

He rubbed the sleep from his eyes. "What happened?"

"I—just come."

"Be right there."

He dressed quickly, scribbled a note for Britt in case she woke up, and slid into the car. As the engine leapt to life, he phoned Jenny.

"Hello?" she said, sounding as drowsy as he had a few minutes earlier.

"It's Rob." He relayed the little their daughter had said.

"Where were Boyer and June when whatever went wrong happened?" Jenny muttered. "Where are you?"

"On my way to pick you up and take you with me to get Maddie. I expect the Wycliffs were asleep like our parents were when we snuck out—if that's what they did." The possibility of his daughter doing exactly that scared him. Anything could've happened. He heard Jenny's sound of alarm.

"Do you think she did? Tell me in the car. I'll throw on some clothes and be ready when you arrive."

~

"I KNOW you're as worried as I am," Jenny told Rob as he sped to pick up their daughter way too fast for her comfort. "But please, ease up on the accelerator. If you get a ticket, it'll only slow us down."

"Don't worry, I'm keeping an eye out for cops. I doubt there are many around at this hour."

"You said something about sneaking out?" Jenny asked, worried sick.

"Call it a wild guess. I know as little as you."

Her cellphone rang. She checked the screen "It's June," she said and answered. "You're on speaker phone—Rob and I are on our way to your house. What happened?"

"Lainey woke us up because Maddie was upset. Apparently, she snuck out to meet her boyfriend after Boyer and I went to bed."

Rob's guess had been dead-on. Ugly thoughts flitted through Jenny's mind. Sick at heart and terrified for her daughter, she hugged her waist and rocked in her seat.

Rob swore loudly, and who could blame him? Needing comfort and also wanting to give him the same, she touched his bicep, which was rock hard with tension.

"We're as upset about this as you are, Rob," June said, sounding both sympathetic and worried. "I wish I were a lighter sleeper. Lainey knew about Maddie's plan, and, of course, didn't tell us. Believe me, she's in big trouble. We're so sorry."

"None of this is your fault," Jenny assured her. She almost wished Maddie had done badly on the test and was still grounded. "We'll be there shortly." She disconnected and glanced at Rob. "What are we going to do?"

"That depends on what happened. Only Maddie knows, and we should encourage her to tell us."

Jenny understood he was warning her not to be angry with their daughter. "For goodness' sake, Rob. I'm not the hysterical type."

"I said that as a reminder for myself, too."

Some of the tension knotting her stomach eased. "Oh. I'm on edge, as you can tell. I know not to yell at her or bombard her with questions." She squared her shoulders. "I'm going to be calm if it kills me."

"I'm not sure I can promise as much. I don't know what Hudson did, but as soon as I do, his parents are going to get a rude wake-up call. If the kid were an adult, I'd punch his lights out."

As big and strong as Rob was, to Jenny's knowledge he'd never punched anyone. "Aren't you the one who wants to find out what happened first?"

He almost smiled. "When did you become the voice of reason?"

"My ex-husband taught me about that."

"He sounds like a great guy."

"He is." The very best. She almost fell in love with him all over again but didn't. Loving him again was a road to nowhere that would end up hurting the two of them and the girls. She refused to let that happen.

"I'm glad you're with me." He clasped her hand.

"Me, too," she said, relieved he couldn't read her mind.

As soon as they pulled up to the house, June opened the door. She and Boyer were in bathrobes and slippers. So was Lainey. Maddie was dressed in the clothes she'd worn under her costume. Sniffling but no longer crying, she glanced from Jenny to Rob, then hung her head. Jenny's heart pounded hard in her chest, and her hands clenched at her sides.

"We'll leave you to talk," June said. "Would you like something warm to drink—coffee or tea? That includes you, Maddie." The three of them declined. "When you leave, the door will lock behind you."

Jenny nodded. "Thanks, June. I'll phone you tomorrow."

She and Rob sat down on the living room sofa, Maddie between them. "Tell us what happened, honey," she said, and tenderly smoothed her daughter's hair behind her ears. Over her head, Rob nodded his approval.

Maddie's tears returned. "Please don't be mad."

Jenny pulled a clean tissue from her purse and handed it to their distraught daughter. "No matter what, we love you and always will," she said, unable to promise she wouldn't be angry.

"Tell us," Rob encouraged, putting his arm around her slumped shoulders.

Maddie stared at her lap. "I made a horrible mistake tonight."

"June—Mrs. Wycliff—told us you snuck out to meet Hudson," Jenny said, proud of her relaxed tone. "What happened?"

"Nothing."

Again, Jenny exchanged glances with Rob. This time, he spoke. "If that were true, you wouldn't be crying."

"Don't make me tell you, Dad. I can't. I won't."

Words that chilled Jenny's blood.

For a few long seconds, no one said a word. Then Rob broke the silence. "Did he force you?" he asked in the deceptively tranquil voice that indicated the opposite. Knowing he was headed for full-fledged fury, Jenny glanced at him and widened her eyes, warning him not to go there.

"No, Dad. Eww."

He heaved a breath that could've been either relief or frustration.

"That's good to know," Jenny soothed, thankful that at least they had the answer to one question. But it didn't mean Maddie hadn't had sex tonight.

She thought back to high school. She and Rob had been a good year older than Maddie when they started talking about having sex. They'd agreed not to and had stuck to that for almost two years, until their powerful hunger for each other had taken over and nothing mattered but being together. They'd both been virgins, and that first time had been beautiful and wondrous for them. Maddie's experience, whatever it was, wasn't like that. "Something happened that's shaken you. Do you want to talk about it?"

"No." Maddie raised her chin. "If you want to ground me again for sneaking out and not explaining, go ahead."

"I won't ground you, I promise."

"But I lied, and I snuck out. I deserve to be back on restriction."

It was almost as if she felt so bad, she wanted to be punished. They seemed to be going in circles and getting nowhere. "It's really late, and I'm sure the Wycliffs are unable to sleep while we're here," she said. "Why don't we all go home and get some much-needed rest."

Maddie nodded. "Which home?"

"You decide," Jenny said, although she longed to be with her daughter, both to comfort her and talk.

"I want to be with Britt."

Jenny's feelings were hurt, but she was glad Maddie and her sister were so close. Neither she nor Rob pointed out that Britt was fast asleep.

Instead of stopping at Jenny's, Rob pulled up at his house.

"Aren't you taking Mom home?" Maddie asked.

"Yes, but first I wanted to get you here. I'll drive her home as soon as you're inside. Alcatraz will be glad to see you. Lock the door behind you. I'll be back soon."

15

O n the way to Jenny's house, nothing was said until Rob pulled into her driveway. "Why didn't you drop me off first?" she asked.

Not ready to answer yet, he exited the car, came around to her side, and opened her door. "Let's go inside." He took her hand, which was even colder than his—stress tended to do that—and they climbed the front steps. Inside, he shrugged his coat off while she did the same. "I need to hold on to you," he said, his voice breaking.

She nodded and touched his cheek. "Me, too. Our poor baby."

He wrapped his arms around her. She was trembling, and it almost undid him.

For long moments, they clung to each other, sharing a warmth and comfort he hadn't experienced in thirteen years. He kissed the top of her head. "You were great tonight, the picture of calm."

"I tried really hard." She looked up at him. "Do you think they had sex?"

"I don't know, but when she almost begged to be grounded ... I can't help but think it happened."

"Same. I hope to God she doesn't get pregnant."

"She won't. You've taught her well." In an effort to comfort her, he smoothed his hands up and down her back. She nestled in close, the way she always had in the days when they were happy. He wanted more with her, foolhardy longings with consequences that would only hurt them both later. With reluctance, he pulled away. "We need rest. I should go."

"I don't know if I'll be able to sleep." She clasped her hands at her waist and fidgeted. "It's your weekend with the girls, but I want to be there for Maddie, too."

The thought of leaving Jenny in the dark during such a traumatic time was a bad idea, and he shook his head. "After what happened, I wouldn't feel comfortable without you. As soon as you're up and dressed tomorrow, come over."

"Even if it's really early? It might be."

"No worries. I'll leave a spare key under the welcome mat."

"That's not a very good hiding place."

"I'll chance it. Besides, we both know how safe it is around here."

She nodded. "What about breakfast? Should we go out?"

"Not the way things stand right now. I have plenty of food at the house."

"Okay, I'll pick up coffees the way the girls like them—pumpkin spice latte for Maddie and a caramel macchiato for Britt. Do you still drink vanilla espresso?"

"When I can. I'll bet you're still into mochas with whipped cream."

"Unfortunately. I should cut down on drinking them." She patted her stomach.

"You look great," he said, with way too much feeling. What had gotten into him? "Dream good things."

"Let's hope we both do."

~

DUE TO WORRY ABOUT MADDIE, Jenny spent the restless night she'd predicted and was up earlier than usual. She texted him to find out if he was awake.

For hours now, he texted back. *Girls are sleeping. Hurry over with those coffees.*

After dressing, she stopped at Rosemary's Breakfast Nook, which was just opening its doors. As one of the few customers so early on a Saturday, she was able to get four coffees and twice as many assorted scones in record time. She arrived at Rob's a little before seven. Inside, Alcatraz greeted her with a happy bark and a wagging tail.

"I don't want you waking up the twins," Rob told him in a low voice. "Time to go out." Already wearing socks, he slid his feet into sneakers, opened the kitchen door that led to the back yard, and ushered his dog into the fenced area to romp and play. Alcatraz slept indoors but also had a doghouse outside complete with a sleeping pad and blanket in case he wanted to snooze.

While Rob was busy with that, Jenny set the coffees and treats on the kitchen counter. Knowing the drinks had cooled down a little, she reheated hers and Rob's in the microwave.

A moment later, he returned and toed out of the shoes.

"It's crisp out there," he said, rubbing his hands together and smelling of cold fresh air. In a flannel shirt, loose, faded jeans, and the socks, he looked relaxed and handsome. But then, he always did. Catching herself in the middle of a dreamy sigh, she compressed her lips and neatly squelched it.

"You okay?" he asked, toying with a frown.

Realizing the corners of her lips turned downward, she gave him a rueful smile. "Trying, but I'm tired and stressed. I warmed our coffees. Here," she said and handed over his.

"Thanks," He raised the drink to his mouth. "I see you brought treats, too."

"Scones."

"Nice. Not a sound from the twins' room. It's good they're both sleeping. They need the rest. They did a lot of talking during the night. I heard crying, too."

"Poor Maddie." Dying to find out something, anything, Jenny asked, "Did you hear what they said?"

He shook his head. "The conversation was private."

"I admire you. I'd have been tempted to eavesdrop."

"But you wouldn't have. That's not you and never has been."

"I guess not. It was something my mother did, though. At least in that way, I'm not like her." She thought a minute. "I recently realized I've truly stopped holding the things she did and the lectures against her anymore. As misguided as she was with me, she did what she thought was right."

"Wow—that's quite an insight. What brought that on?"

"I was at my dad's for dinner the other night, and we talked about it. Speaking of Dad, I finally met Adelle."

"After he's been seeing her for how long? Sounds like things are getting serious."

"I think so. I really like her. The relationship between her and my dad is special. They're a true example of mature love and knowing how to handle whatever comes at them well. I invited him to bring her to Thanksgiving dinner."

"Great. I'll get to meet her when I pick up the girls in the afternoon." Rob sipped his drink again, with a gusto that included smacking his lips and letting out a sigh of pleasure. He always had savored that first morning cup of coffee.

"Speaking of family," he went on, "my parents wanted me to bring the girls over for brunch at their house Sunday. I said yes, but in light of what's happened I think I'll postpone. They'll see each other Thanksgiving. Can't believe that's less than a month from now." He checked his watch. "I'll phone them in a bit, when they're likely to be awake. It's good that Maddie talked to Britt last night. She has to confide in someone. I'm glad they're sleeping later than we did. They just might sleep the day away."

"Let them," Jenny said. "Teens need lots of rest. Let's leave their drinks on the counter. When they're up and ready, they can nuke them. As for me, I could use another cup. Plain old, regular coffee with half and half—if you don't mind making a pot."

"Not at all. I have a hunch I'll be guzzling the stuff all day."

The coffee was gurgling when her stomach growled. "I say we go with breakfast," she said.

"Deal. Give me five to call the parents." He paused. "I don't think I'll mention you're here. No telling what they might think." Moments later, he put his phone away. "I let them know we can't make it this week, and that we're looking forward to seeing them Thanksgiving. Cheese omelets okay?"

"Yes, please. You make those. I'll do the bacon and warm the scones."

The kitchen soon filled with the smells of coffee, butter, bacon, and two piping hot scones. Jenny's mouth watered. They sat down at the table to eat. "This is delicious," she said moments later. "You make the best omelets."

"One of my specialties. I like this crisp bacon, and these scones are great." After that, neither of them spoke much until Rob set his fork down. "Do you realize we haven't argued once since those massages? And to think, I considered bowing out of it."

"A good thing you didn't. If you had, nothing would've changed." No kisses, and she wouldn't be yearning for him. She wasn't about to point that out. He didn't mention it, either. "Since then, we've been on the verge of getting into it a few times, but we somehow managed not to. A welcome change from picking at each other."

"Sure is. If we keep this up, people will talk." He looked her straight in the eyes, his gaze so bright and warm, she went a little haywire, and the longing to lean across the table and kiss him was almost overwhelming. Almost.

"Let them." She tore her gaze away and managed to contain the urge. "Any fool with that idea will soon learn that we're not happening, not the way they think, because we won't let it. Getting back together would be a disaster I wouldn't want to repeat."

Grimacing as if the idea gave him a bad taste, he brushed his hand over his fade. "But like I said at the firehouse last night, I still want you. I realize that makes me sound certifiable, but I don't have much control over my emotions." He shot her another of the hot-eyed looks that were so irresistible. "Especially when you look at me like you want me, too."

Holding onto her composure was already difficult enough. "Don't say that," she pleaded without much conviction.

"Why not? It's the truth." He set his fork down, got up, and started toward her.

"We can get past this if we both fight it," she said, but he pulled her to her feet and cupped her face in his warm hands, and she was lost.

16

Rob's mouth was so eager, his arms wrapped tightly around Jenny as if he wanted to meld her to him. She caught fire. Before long, they were frantically groping each other, hands under tops, lower bodies pressed tightly together.

Hardly aware what she was doing, she arched her back and pushed her breasts out, a silent plea to touch her. He cupped them, then slid his fingers inside her bra.

"I want you so much," he whispered.

His hands, oh, his clever hands. He hadn't forgotten what she liked. She stepped away to remove her top and bra.

Suddenly they heard voices.

"The twins are up," she murmured, passion fleeing.

Rob snorted a laugh. "And me about to swell out of my fly."

"You'd better sit down."

"You need to smooth your top and your hair. You look like—like you just had sex."

Thank goodness they hadn't. She did the best she

could, smoothing her hair by feel and straightening her pullover. "Do I look okay?"

"You always do. Your cheeks are pink, though. Maybe they won't notice."

"Before they come in here, remember I promised June I'd touch bases today? I don't know what to say."

"The truth—that we haven't learned much. Let's hope Maddie opens up to us this morning."

"Fingers crossed. Do you think Britt knew she was going to sneak out?"

"As close as they are, I wouldn't be surprised. But don't get your hopes up. We can't force either of them to talk, but we can feed them."

The twins wandered into the kitchen, Maddie in a long-sleeve T and pajama bottoms, and Britt in a two-piece pajama set. Both barefoot. Their feet must be ice-cold.

"Good morning, sleepyheads," Jenny said, fighting the urge to suggest they get their slippers. She wasn't in the mood for rolled eyes or worse.

Maddie frowned. "What are you doing here, Mom? This is our weekend with Dad."

As if she and Rob didn't know that. "We thought it'd be nice to have breakfast together. We haven't done that in such a long time." She made herself smile. "Friendly and comfortable, not tense. That's a promise."

Maddie fiddled with her hair. "After what I did last night, you shouldn't be so nice."

Tell us what happened, Jenny wanted to prompt, but the slight shake of Rob's head stopped her. How had he known what she'd been about to ask?

Britt gave her sister an anxious glance. "I'm glad both Mom and Dad are here, and that they're getting along."

"I appreciate that, Britt," Jenny said. "We're trying."

Rob almost smiled. "You noticed. How are you feeling today, Maddie?"

Her mouth wobbled, and Jenny was sure she'd start crying. But no, in a surprise move, she raised her chin. "I'm doing okay. And don't ask me what happened," she added as if she'd read their minds.

She had no idea how strong she was. If only she'd open up ... "We won't," Jenny assured her. "But know that if you want to talk to either me, your dad, or both of us, we're here. I give you my word we'll listen without judgment."

Her suffering daughter ignored her. "Looks like you already ate," she said, sounding angry as she nodded at the empty plates.

Jenny was used to the mood changes of fifteen-year-old girls. "We were hungry and assumed you'd sleep in. We didn't want to wait for you to get up, so we went ahead and had breakfast."

"Now that you're awake, how about I make you each one of my famous omelets?" Rob said, forming quote marks with his fingers. He pushed to his feet.

No sign of an arousal, Jenny noted with relief. "They'll go well with the coffees and scones I picked up at Rosemary's," she told the twins. "I got your favorites. Everything's cold now, but it'll heat fast in the microwave."

"I'll start with coffee," Britt said, licking her lips as she headed for the cups Jenny had set on the counter. "By the way, I have an Ultimate Frisbee game this afternoon."

"That's right, and thanks for the reminder," Jenny said. "I'll be there."

Rob nodded. "I will, too—after I drop you off at your art class, Maddie."

"I'm not going today."

Not wanting to argue, Jenny invited her to the game. She didn't say yes but didn't turn down the offer, either. She no longer seemed to be on the verge of anger or tears.

"How long have you been here, Mom?" she asked, shooting a curious glance at her and Rob.

Trying hard not to blush, not that she had any control over that, Jenny told her. "Awhile. We figured you were both tired and it's Saturday. We wanted you to sleep in, and you did."

"You were awfully quiet in here," Britt said, on the verge of a smirk that rivaled her twin's.

Mortified they might have guessed what she and Rob had been up to, Jenny forced a nonchalant shrug. "When two people are eating and trying to get along, it's best to keep the conversation to a minimum."

"If you say so." This time they both snorted.

Jenny didn't dare glance at Rob for fear they'd figure things out. "Your dad let Alcatraz out earlier. I think I'll let him in now—if you don't mind, Rob."

"Do it," he said, already pulling the egg carton from the fridge.

After Alcatraz greeted the girls, he settled down near the stove, no doubt hoping for a bite of whatever dropped on the floor.

Meanwhile, the twins whispered and continued scrutinizing Jenny and their father.

"That's enough, you two," Rob ordered in a no-nonsense voice. "The stove is hot and I'm ready to cook. Do you want omelets or not?"

"I do," Britt said. "Ham and cheese, please."

"I don't have any ham. Will bacon do instead?"

"That's what I want," Maddie said, and Britt nodded that she was fine with the same.

For a moment, neither of the girls said much. Then Maddie eyed Jenny. "You can go home now, Mom. This is our time to be with Dad."

Stung, Jenny nodded. "Okay. I'll see you at the game this afternoon. Otherwise, tomorrow night."

On the drive home, her frustration poured out. She pounded on the steering wheel and howled at the world. Would Maddie never open up? She doubted their daughter would tell her anything. Maybe Rob would learn something. Getting left out hurt. Nothing to do but contact June and hear what she'd learned, then wait and cross her fingers to find out more.

THE REST of Saturday was relatively calm. Shortly after Rob took Britt to her Ultimate Frisbee game, Jenny showed up. She enjoyed the game as much as he did. He made an effort to act as if nothing had changed between them, greeting her with a casual nod.

But something had.

In less than twenty-four hours, they'd crossed a boundary they'd agreed not to. He didn't lose control often, and his lack of self-restraint bothered him. Especially when the girls were in the house. How careless was that? But the pull between them had been too strong to resist. This worried him, and he swore he wouldn't go there again.

Despite the cold and rain threatening at any moment, Britt's team played well and won.

During the game, he and Jenny conferred occasionally about the action as they often did. In lower voices, they discussed Maddie. He hadn't been able to talk her into going to art class, which she normally loved. Jenny was as concerned as he was. "I sure wish she'd open up," he said. "Did you talk to June?"

Jenny nodded. "She had nothing new to report, and Lainey claimed she didn't know anything, either. So frustrating."

"If Maddie's still this way tomorrow, you and I should talk to her when I bring her, Britt, and Alcatraz to your place." He thought for a minute. "Why don't I come in the late afternoon instead of at dinnertime. By then, she'll have had another day to deal with whatever happened and might be ready to tell us."

For the remainder of the afternoon and all day Sunday, both girls spent much of their time holed up in the bedroom, talking, doing homework, and who knew what else.

"Why are we going to Mom's early?" Britt asked as he drove to Jenny's Sunday afternoon.

"No reason," he said, careful to sound nonchalant.

He could feel her eyes on him. "Did she invite you to dinner?"

"No." He leashed Alcatraz and headed for the front door. Once inside, both Britt and Maddie gave them quizzical looks. They seemed to be watching him and Jenny closely, especially Maddie. "You guys are up to something," she said, narrowing her eyes. "Why don't you just tell us?"

"Your mom and I want to talk to you privately. Would you mind going upstairs, Britt?"

Britt telegraphed an unreadable look to her sister, who clamped her lips, then teared up. "It's okay, Britt."

"Let's sit down," Rob suggested as Britt disappeared up the stairs.

Jenny nodded. "Where to you want to do this, Maddie?"

"The kitchen table, I guess." Their daughter swallowed audibly. "Can I have a pop?"

"Of course," Jenny said. "Help yourself. You, too, Rob—unless you'd prefer tea or decaf? It's too late in the day for me to have caffeine."

Drinks in hand, they sat down on the same side of the table, which seated six, Maddie between them. In tacit agreement, both he and Jenny kept their mouths shut, letting their daughter control the conversation.

It took a while before she said anything. "This is so embarrassing and awful." She studied the half-empty pop bottle with an intensity that let Rob know she couldn't bear to look at their faces.

"Your dad and I love you so much," Jenny said, reaching out to briefly cup her daughter's shoulder. "We want to hear whatever you have to say—if you're ready to tell us."

"I think I might be," Maddie said, sniffling and fiddling with her sleeve.

Jenny handed her a tissue. Then they waited.

Maddie blew her nose. "Hudson and I have been talking about sex for a while now."

Rob sensed his ex stiffening and was right there with her. "Okay," he said, working hard to keep his tone and expression neutral when he wanted to spit nails. He didn't want to spook her.

"Like I told you the other night, I waited until everyone was asleep before I snuck out to meet him." She fiddled with the pop bottle. "As soon as I climbed into the van, I changed my mind."

"Van?" Rob asked, barely corralling his temper. Over Maddie's bowed head, Jenny widened her eyes and shook her head, silently warning him not to go overboard. He forced himself to be calm. "Go on, Maddie."

Witnessing her pain and misery hurt more than almost anything he'd experienced in life, and he barely curtailed his own wail. Staring at something only she could see, Maddie didn't notice. "His older brother said we could use it and parked it around the block. As soon as I was in the van and saw that mattress ..." She swallowed audibly. "I didn't want to lie on that thing with him," she blubbered. "I didn't want to be in the van, either." She paused to blow her nose. "I thought I was ready for sex, but I'm not."

Rob wanted to slam his fist on the table. Instead, he put his hands on his thighs and squeezed them into hard fists.

"It's good that you know that about yourself," Jenny consoled, "and I understand why that would make you cry."

Following her lead, he again stifled his rage. "The other night, you said he didn't force you," he reminded Maddie, hoping against hope she hadn't been coerced into giving in.

"He didn't, Dad, but he was mad that I wouldn't have sex. He called me a tease and wouldn't even look at me. As soon as I got out of the van, he slammed the door hard." She was still blubbering. "It felt like he only wanted me for sex, and that makes me feel awful. What if he tells his friends?"

She was worried about what others might think. That made sense.

Jenny had clamped her jaw, but her soft tone didn't reflect what she must be feeling. "I'm so sorry, honey. If he says anything, it only makes him look worse."

"Your mom's right about that. Where does Hudson live?"

Looking panicky, Maddie shook her head. "I don't want to tell you."

"Why not? It's not like I'm going to his house." At least, not yet. "I'm at the firehouse until Wednesday morning."

"Please don't do anything, Dad. I said I wanted to have sex with him, then I backed out. It's my fault he got mad."

"Not true," he told her. "If he was a decent kid and really cared about you, he'd have treated you better. You deserve someone as special as you are. He's not it."

"I know that now." Maddie sniffled.

"That's my girl."

He put his arm around her shoulders. From the other side, so did Jenny. Their arms overlapped and they clasped hands, which Rob found comforting.

"You were brave to tell us," she said. "You're stronger than you think, and I admire you so much."

"Why?" Tears again and time for a fresh tissue.

"Because you are. You walked away from Hudson instead of giving in to keep him from getting mad, and you told your dad and me what happened. That takes real courage."

"You did the right thing," Rob agreed. "I'm proud to have such a brave daughter."

His words only made her cry harder. "I don't want to go to school tomorrow," she sobbed. "Hudson's in my homeroom and I'm scared to see him."

Jenny nodded. "That's understandable."

"What would you do, Mom?"

Rob's ex gave him a *help* look, and he chimed in. "That's a good question. Your mom has always been strong. What would you do, Jenny?"

"If it were me, I'd go to school with my head held high and show Hudson I'm not afraid of him—even if

I was. You have lots of good friends. Maybe you'll feel better if you talk to them."

"Britt knows the whole story, but she has a different homeroom. Lainey's in mine, but she doesn't know everything that happened. I guess I'll call her tonight."

Rob approved. "That's a good plan. I have faith in you."

"Thanks, Dad."

"You're welcome." His eyes a little wet, too, he stood. "I should go home and get ready for tomorrow. If you want to talk at all, I'll listen."

"Or me," Jenny added. "It's time I fixed dinner. Why don't you go upstairs and tell Britt to come down? Then you can both help."

"Do you want to stay, Dad?" Maddie's eyes widened hopefully.

He did, but that probably wasn't a good idea. "I can't. I'll go upstairs to say goodbye to Britt and tell her she's needed in the kitchen."

That done, he left.

17

At the station Monday, Rob met the guys in the firehouse kitchen for breakfast, which each man brought for himself. As always, they schmoosed about the weekend. Much of the conversation centered on the firehouse's Halloween party.

Only a handful of guys had volunteered. "Our party was a big success," Adam said for the benefit of the rest. "We had a great turnout and sold a ton of calendars. I must've autographed twenty or thirty." Collecting crew member's autographs had always been popular. He shook his head. "We're nearing the end of the year, yet people still want our John Hancocks."

"I hear that," Rob said. "I know I'm not the only one who'll be glad when it ends."

"Doesn't mean people will stop asking," Tony reminded him. "I get tired of women wanting me to call them, even when I tell them I'm taken."

Having never been one to enjoy the minor celebrity status resulting from his photo plastered on the calendar, Rob agreed. "I sure am tired of all the attention."

"Cool of Jenny to show up and help," Gus commented. "She hasn't done that in a while, not since your girls were little."

"I was surprised she wanted to, and I think she enjoyed it," Rob said. "The more, the merrier, right?"

Gus zeroed in on him. "Are you two getting along now?" Curious looks all around.

Oh, yeah, and none of their business. "At the moment."

"Hey, that's something, right?" Gus said, scratching his chin. "I like massages as much as anyone, but it can't have been that."

No doubt, he'd heard about that from the guys who'd been at poker night. Skipping over how the couple's massage had in fact changed everything, Rob managed a casual shrug. "The massages were a big help. That and making up our minds to get along. So far so good. Let's hope it lasts." Breakfast over, he collected his trash and tossed it. "Time to do the morning chores."

This being Ethan, Daniel, and Rob's week for the paramedic rotation, they were responsible for the morning inspection of the engines, ambulances, and aid cars. They also handled medical calls and conducted safety classes in various places around town. He glanced at his two counterparts. "Care to join me, gentlemen?"

The moniker caused snickers from everyone and took the heat off him.

But during inventory checks on each of the vehicles, Daniel revived the conversation. "I heard you and Jenny disappeared at the same time during the party." He flashed a knowing grin. "You sly dog."

Enough already. Rob eyed him. "What's that supposed to mean? You weren't even there."

"I was," Ethan said. "You two left the room at the

same time, and you came back a few minutes apart, both looking pleased with yourselves. I'm not the only one who noticed." He also grinned.

Crap. "Knock it off," Rob warned.

Ethan ignored that. "We weren't the ones who disappeared. Anyone with eyes could see how well you two got along that night. I'm happy for you, and I want info. What's going on with you and her?"

No point pretending there was nothing to explain. Heck, Rob wasn't sure what the changes between Jenny and him meant. He laced up his sneakers. "You're right—at the moment, we're getting along really well. Whether it lasts or not is anyone's guess."

"I'm not the only guy who hopes your truce continues for a long time," Ethan said. "Who knows, you might get together again."

Rob was all for peace between them and was strongly attracted to her, but that was the extent of his feelings. "Don't even go there. It's only been a week or so since we decided to get along better. We haven't gone near the idea of getting back together. That'd be a bad move. Too much baggage, you know? It won't happen."

But they were definitely enjoying each other, especially in the physical sense. Amazing how quickly passion flared between them, as hot as it once had been. After all this time, too.

Most of his feelings were related to that. He had no idea what it meant or where it would lead, but he intended to savor it while it lasted. "We're serious about getting along better. Dealing with fifteen-year-old twins is a huge challenge, and for our sakes and theirs, we need to present a unified front. Right now, Maddie's having a rough time, nothing I want to share." He wouldn't feel right talking about that. "I hope our less tense relationship will make life easier for her and Britt. For their sakes, I'd appreciate it if you didn't speculate or spread any rumors about Jenny and me."

Chores done, they headed to the locker room to work out. Suddenly, the intercom sounded. The dispatcher came on with a 911 alert about a possible cardiac arrest.

"That's us," Daniel said, and they jumped into the ambulance. Ethan drove. As they headed off, talk about Jenny and him ended at last.

AFTER SEEING the girls off Monday morning, Jenny hoped Maddie survived the day without suffering through too much discomfort and embarrassment. She fed and watered Alcatraz and the other boarded dogs. Alicia was due to arrive soon, a good thing, as Jenny needed to confide in her. After they finished later this morning, she'd head to Fashion Dogs for the weekly meeting.

As soon as Alicia arrived and they leashed the animals, they set out for the doggie daycare a few blocks away, where the daycare regulars waited for their weekday morning walk. It was a brisk, chilly day, and both Jenny and Alicia bundled up in parkas and gloves. Jenny tucked her hair into her wool cap; Alicia wore earmuffs and let her shoulder-length hair hang free. No fan of the cold, they both tolerated it, while the dogs were thrilled to be outside, their tails wagging with eagerness.

"How was your weekend, Alicia?" she asked as they headed out at a brisk pace the animals seemed to relish. "You went to a Halloween party with Piet, right?" The Danish boyfriend Alicia had been seeing for months.

"Yes, and we had so much fun." She beamed a million-dollar grin, and Jenny couldn't help but smile.

"What did you dress up as?"

"Cruella de Vil, which is funny considering how much I love dogs." Alicia cast a warm look at the happy canines around her. "Did you hear that, guys? I love you and would never think of making coats out of your fur! Piet was a Viking. He looked smokin' hot."

Courtesy of the fast pace, Jenny was breathing hard. She pictured the buff Piet decked out in a tunic and pants. "I'm imagining that now, but that's not why I'm breathless. These dogs are giving me a real workout. Did you get a photo or two of him?"

"A bunch. I'll send you a couple later. I'm out of breath, too. How about your costume? You helped out at the fire station, right?"

Jenny nodded. "I went as Rapunzel. You should've seen my wig! So ugly." She smiled. "It was fun. Noisy, though. The place was packed with parents and kids."

"So you and Rob got along?"

Much more than that. "Surprisingly, we did."

"Those massages last week must've worked."

"Maybe a little too well."

Alicia's eyes widened. "Are you saying what I think you are?"

Time to confide in her friend. "Things are starting to heat up, but I don't know what will happen."

"You like each other again? That's great."

"Our feelings are mostly physical—I don't know about the rest. And don't you dare tell a soul about anything we talk about this morning."

"Not even Piet. Cross my heart. How physical are you so far?"

"Nowhere near to having sex, but I'm thinking about it."

"Wow. And after all this time apart. It happens with divorced couples. Not long after my parents split up, they got back together, but only for a few months." She made a face. "The thought of them having sex isn't something I want to think about."

"I'm sure Britt and Maddie would be thoroughly grossed out. After being divorced thirteen years, I never thought I'd feel this way about Rob. I have no idea if what's going on with us is anything like what happened with your parents. All I know is, he's every bit as interested in the physical thing."

"Whatever happens, keep me updated. Speaking of Maddie and Britt, did they have a good time at their party?"

"Britt did." Wanting to talk about Maddie and get Alicia's perspective, Jenny let out a weighty sigh that had nothing to do with the pace of their walk. "Maddie, though? Things started off okay, but then around midnight she snuck out to meet her boyfriend. That didn't go well."

Alicia's mouth formed and O of alarm. "What happened?"

Jenny shared the entire story, beginning with the tearful, early morning-phone call their daughter had made to Rob. "She refused to tell us about the van and the nasty things Hudson said but changed her mind last night. We finally talked it through then."

"Poor Maddie. It could've turned out a lot worse, though. I've known a friend or two where—well, bad things happened."

"She's lucky but also traumatized. I worry she'll have a hard time getting over what happened. I guess if that plays out, we'll find a good therapist for her. She went to school today worried about what people would say and how she'd react when she saw Hudson."

"I don't know her well, but she always struck me as a strong girl. I'm sure her friends and the people who care about her will stand up for her."

Jenny crossed her fingers. They returned to the doggie daycare pick-up site to drop off the canines from their walk, then headed home and let the boarded dogs into their kennels, which were insulated and outfitted with bedding and blankets, and thanks to the generosity of her father.

Alicia left. Inside, Jenny brewed a cup of cinnamon spice tea and checked her phone for messages. Nothing from Maddie or Britt, a good sign, she hoped. Soon enough, she'd find out.

18

At the firehouse following a hectic morning and afternoon, Rob completed the paperwork on the cardiac arrest patient, an older, overweight male who smoked. He also wondered about Maddie. He hadn't heard anything from her or Jenny. By now, she'd be on the bus and headed for home. He texted her. *How are you? Did you make it through the day okay?*

When she didn't reply, he phoned Jenny.

"Hi," she said, sounding pleased to hear from him.

He grinned at that and imagined kissing the smile right off her face—and more. Then he pushed the arousing thought away. "Any word on Maddie?"

"No, and I take that as a positive sign. I'll let you know what she has to say once she's home. How are you? Is this a slow day?"

"So-so. This morning, we had a heart attack victim who's going to make it. That took a while. Later, there was a fire in a vacant building. Then a middle-school kid with a bad temper kicked a locker and jammed his toe really hard."

"Ouch. That must've been some kick."

"Yep. Maybe he'll think twice next time about how

to deal with frustration." He paused. "Here's something you won't like. I got blitzed this morning about Friday night. People saw us leave the lobby together and then come back separately. You should've heard the snarky comments."

"You're right, I don't like that. It's so embarrassing."

"I shrugged it off. What else could I do? It was—" An alert sounded, and Sarah McCone's voice filled the air. "Gotta go," he said and disconnected. In no time, he was suited up. Ethan was busy with something else, so Liam drove. Rob sat shotgun, with Daniel in the back.

As it turned out, a fire alarm at Orchard High had triggered, summoning the GLFD as well as a team of officers from the Guff Lake PD. Rob suspected the call was a false alarm, yet during the entire ride, he thought about his daughters. They were likely safe, but his apprehension level skyrocketed.

The entire school—six hundred students, plus teachers, admins, and anyone else who'd been in the building—had amassed on the football field to wait for the inspection and the all-clear. He caught sight of Maddie and some of the friends he recognized. Britt stood nearby with another group. He knew when they spotted him because they pointed him out and their friends stared at him. He also noticed Theo and nodded at him, and Hudson, who he narrow-eyed for being such a jackass to Maddie. The boy turned red and glanced down. Rob decided the time was right for a call to his parents. Maddie might not like it, but they needed to know.

After a quick conversation with the principal, who informed them that one of the sophomore boys had pulled the fire alarm as a prank, the fire crew and officers swarmed inside for a thorough search of the building. Standard protocol.

Some thirty minutes later, the students and faculty were allowed back into the school. The boy responsible headed directly to the principal's office to wait for his parents, who were quickly summoned, and a likely temporary expulsion.

Rob considered peeking in at his daughters to say hi, but he didn't want to embarrass them or further disrupt classes that had already been interrupted. On the drive back to the station, the crew talked about the stupid move of the boy and the trouble he was in.

At the station again, he phoned Jenny.

"You're back already?" she said.

"The call lasted almost two hours. Some kid at Orchard High pulled the fire alarm. Man, is he in for it."

"Orchard High? Did you see the girls?"

"Only for a minute while they and the rest of the people at the school waited outside for us to do the all-clear. I spotted Hudson, too, and gave him the evil eye."

"Your evil eye is powerful. I'll bet he was embarrassed."

"Beet red and a little intimidated."

"As well he should be," Jenny said.

"I think the time is right for one of us to get in touch with his parents. I'll do that, unless you'd rather."

"Why don't you? Maddie will probably get mad, but I think it's a good idea. When are you planning to tell her?"

"After I talk to them."

"Sounds good. Back to the boy who pulled the fire alarm. Kids that age don't think things through. I wonder if he's someone we know?"

"No idea, but I'll bet the girls will tell you." Rob checked his watch. "They should be home soon. Lots to do here. I should go. I hope Maddie had an okay day. Text after you talk to her?"

"I will." She paused a moment. "Do you realize we've been in contact with each other a lot lately? Like we used to."

He had to think about that. "You mean staying in touch throughout the day and not arguing?" Before they'd called it quits, back when he was a rookie.

"That's it exactly. Our relationship is changing for the better. As much as I regret the fight we had at Harvey's, it forced us to rethink the way we interact. That led to the massages, and here we are."

"I hadn't thought about it that way." The experience had definitely been the catalyst, which was both good and bad. Bad because like it or not, it'd reawakened his physical attraction to her. He wanted her the way he hadn't wanted a woman in a long time. She seemed to feel the same about him. What a shame—with their track record, acting on their feelings guaranteed an outcome he'd rather not face.

"You're awfully quiet Rob. What are you thinking?"

Plain and simple, he wanted to have sex with her. He wasn't about to admit it or do anything crazy and give in to his hunger. They needed to talk more about that when he had time. "Right now, I need to finish this paperwork and restock the ambulance and aid cars, but I'll call you back later tonight after I talk to Hudson's folks."

～

ABOUT A HALF-HOUR after talking to Rob, while waiting for Maddie to get home—Britt had Ultimate

Frisbee practice and would get a ride home with her carpool—Jenny thought about her ex-husband and how much she liked being with him and having civil conversations. How much she liked him, period. She'd almost forgotten what a great kisser he was. She wanted to kiss him again a whole bunch of times, and let it lead to where it may. In the past, their physical relationship had been wonderful. It'd been forever since she'd had sex that good. It was never that great with the other guys she'd been with.

Here she was, yearning for him all over again. Giving into her hunger would be the worst because when they parted ways, which they would, the girls would be devastated. So would she and likely Rob, too.

Why was she even thinking about that? Liking each other and wanting sex didn't mean they belonged together. She was positive he felt the same way. After all, they were both scarred from the fallout of their failed marriage. Something to think about, but not now. In the mood to cook, she focused on dinner and a dessert sure to please the girls.

Maddie came in and went straight to the fridge. "Wash your hands first," Jenny reminded her.

Grumbling, she complied, then fished through the fridge for cheese. She got out the crackers and sat down to eat. "What's for dinner tonight?"

"Chicken and noodle casserole. I'll make peas, too."

"Oh, good. What about dessert? Whatever you're baking smells yummy."

"One of your favorites—pumpkin oatmeal bread with chocolate chips."

"Yum." Maddie licked her lips, then devoured the

snack like a girl who hadn't eaten in a while. A care-free girl.

Not a word about Hudson or school. That had to be good news, right? Apparently, it was up to Jenny to start the conversation. "I heard some boy pulled a fire alarm at your school today."

Maddie swallowed her mouthful. "How did you know?"

"Your dad called and told me."

"He did?" She flashed the curious, pleased expression she'd been wearing lately, and Jenny knew she had high hopes for her and Rob. She needed to put a stop to that. Something to discuss with him.

"It was at your school, and I guess he thought I should know," she explained. "So who was the boy who did it?"

"Tam Burns."

"The skinny kid with the curly hair who used to live down the block?"

"That's the one. He did it as a prank, trying to impress his goofy friends." She *hmphed* and shook her head. "What an idiot."

Jenny agreed. "I'll bet he's in big trouble now."

"Suspended for five days. His parents will probably ground him forever."

"Tough way to learn a lesson. How was homeroom today?"

Maddie stopped eating. "Lainey and a few other friends gave Hudson and his friends dirty looks. He pretended not to notice, but I think it bothered him. I kept my head up and acted like everything was fine. But I'm boiling mad, and he knows it."

"Sounds like you did great."

"I don't feel that way."

"Well, I'm proud of you. Trust me, you'll get over

this." With any luck, she'd have a new boyfriend soon, one who liked her because of who she was, not for what he thought he could get from her.

"Thanks, Mom."

"Your dad wants to hear about it, but I think he's pretty busy right now. Do you want to call him after dinner?"

"I guess. Or you can tell him." Maddie almost smiled.

"I'm sure he'd rather hear about it from you."

"I'll do it later." She stood and loaded her dishes into the dishwasher. "I'm going upstairs to do some homework." Partway upstairs, she paused and looked at Jenny over her shoulder. "Do you think we could invite Dad to dinner sometime?" While Jenny pondered that, Maddie went on. "You had breakfast at his house the other day. It's our turn. It'd be fun." She paused. "Or maybe you and he should go out together. Britt and I can take care of ourselves."

Her expectant expression was worrisome. Heartbreaking. "I don't know that your father and I want to do that. We're on good terms right now, but who knows how long it'll last. Don't think we're getting back together. We're not."

Maddie looked stricken. "I wasn't thinking that, Mom. I just want us all to get along." She stomped up the stairs. Moments later, the bedroom door slammed behind her. Jenny flinched.

Moody, jumping from subject to subject—both were tiresome. No telling what Rob would think about that. She texted him the gist and told him to expect a call from Maddie later.

19

That evening, Rob texted Jenny. *Talked to Hudson's dad. Up for a call?*

Moments later, she replied. *Now is good. I think Maddie's still awake.*

"Hi," she answered when he phoned. "This is a perfect time. I'm reading in bed, but not at all sleepy."

He pictured her in a long sleeve pajama set, the kind she'd taken to wearing after the birth of the twins. Prior to that, she'd slept in a loose nightie thing easy to push out of the way or shed when they made love. Which had been often and always excellent ... Now he was getting aroused. What a dolt. Warning himself to knock it off, he shut out the thought.

"What happened when you talked to Hudson's dad —not his mother, too?" she said. "Wait, tell me about your earlier conversation with Maddie. She said she'd call you. I assume you talked to Britt, too?"

"They didn't say anything to you about that?"

"I haven't seen them since you talked to them— they're in their room and I'm in mine."

"Right. Maddie told me about her day and how she'd snubbed Hudson. She sounded really proud of herself and I said I admired her courage. Then I told her what you already know—that I scowled at him out there on the football field, and how his face got all red and he looked down at the ground. And that a dirty look was the least I could give him."

"How did she react to that?"

"She groaned like she was embarrassed, but I think she was secretly pleased. By the way, the reason I didn't talk to his mother, too, is that she's a nurse and works the night shift. Britt was full of chatter about Ultimate Frisbee practice and her science and English Lit classes. She's doing so well. They may be twins, but they're very different from each other."

"We've both known since the day they were born. Britt looked calmly around, and Maddie let out a cry that probably shook everyone in the maternity ward."

He grinned at the memory. "I remember." He heard the rustle of covers and imagined Jenny snuggling in, and almost wished he was there with her. At the same time, he was glad he wasn't.

"I think that in her own way, Maddie's doing all right. Did she mention us?"

"You and me?" Rob frowned. "I'm not following."

"Let me fill you in. First, she suggested I invite you to dinner. Then she changed her mind and said you and I should go out instead, just the two of us."

"She did? What'd Britt say?"

"She wasn't home yet. If you could've seen the hopeful look on her face ... I worry she's thinking we're getting back together. She was too little to remember how bad things were between us when we decided to split up."

"Something to be thankful for." As much as Rob wanted to be with Jenny, he wasn't foolish enough to consider anything close to getting back together. He scrubbed the back of his neck. "Us together again? That's a definite no-no."

"Exactly why I set her straight and told her it wasn't going to happen."

"Next time I talk to her, I'll do the same."

"They'll be going to sleep soon. I assume you reached Hudson's dad? Give me a quick summary of what happened, then I'll put Maddie on."

"He seems like a decent guy. I'm sure he'll update his wife when she's home. He was plenty steamed about his son and will make him call Maddie after school tomorrow and apologize. I expect he'll be grounded."

"Good to know, but I doubt Maddie wants to talk to him. Hang on." She padded down the hall and knocked on the girls' door. "Maddie, your dad's on the phone."

"But we talked after school."

"Yeah," Britt said.

"He has something else to tell you, Maddie." Jenny handed over her phone. "When you finish, bring this back to me."

Five minutes later, her daughter tromped down the hall as if she was mad. Uh-oh. "Dad told Hudson's father what happened. Now Hudson has to call me and apologize tomorrow." She made a face.

"I'm putting the phone on speaker mode, Rob, so you can hear. Dad had to, honey. Hudson's parents needed to know. I'm sorry if that upset you."

"I'm kinda glad you did it, Dad. I don't really want Hudson to call, but I guess it'll be okay."

"Anything else you want to add, Rob?" Jenny asked.

"Only that I'm relieved he's going to call. Good night, Maddie."

"Night, Dad. Night, Mom." She headed back up the stairs.

"That went surprisingly well," Jenny said as she headed back to bed.

"Much better than I imagined." Rob yawned. It was getting late and he was ready to call it a night and turn in. He opened his mouth to say so, but entirely different words spilled out all on their own. "Want to hear something crazy? Even though I totally agree with you about us never getting back together, I still want to see you." The words hung in the air. Not wanting her to get the wrong idea, he quickly went on. "I guess I could come to dinner, if we keep things casual like we did at my house over breakfast. Like we're friends."

"That didn't happen till we heard the girls heading toward the kitchen. Before that, we were doing a lot more than making friendly conversation."

"True," he said, wanting her right now. "Suddenly, I'm not thinking about sleep."

He heard the soft exhale he knew so well, a sign she was on the same wavelength, and almost groaned with longing.

"What are you thinking?" she said, her voice soft and low.

"The same thing as you."

And there it was. Sex.

Her swallow was loud enough to hear on the phone. "I don't know, Rob."

"It doesn't have to mean anything. We're not crazy teens anymore, we're two adults who want each other physically." Lately, he wanted her too much to care about anything else.

"Can I get back to you?"

"Sure. Good night and sweet dreams."

He had a hunch his would be hot.

~

AFTER A NIGHT of restlessness and yearning, Jenny made up her mind. When Alicia showed up Tuesday morning, she discussed the decision with her friend. "I told you I've been thinking about sex with Rob," she admitted. "Would that be so bad?"

Alicia didn't hesitate. "Heck, no. We all need physical gratification. Just be sure you're on the same page about what that means. You don't want to get hurt."

Jenny recalled the other night's conversation with Rob. "We have no interest in getting back together. This would be purely physical." Then and there, she hatched out a plan. "I think I'll call Frankie and ask her to come help you tomorrow morning. I'll go over to Rob's and deliver Alcatraz to him in person so he doesn't have to come here."

"Service with a smile and side benefits, too. I'm sure he'll appreciate it."

Within moments after contacting Frankie, the girl replied that she'd be there.

Wednesday morning, Jenny texted him while the girls were waking up and she was still in bed. *Something different today—I'll bring Alcatraz to you. Unless you have a detail job lined up.* She crossed her fingers and sent it.

She was about to step into the shower when he replied. *Daniel agreed to take my appointment this morning. I have another scheduled midafternoon. Can you come early?*

As soon as Alicia and Frankie arrive.

20

There was only one reason Jenny had invited herself over, Rob figured—she'd decided about sex. Must be good news. Otherwise, she'd have stayed home. He'd planned to join a handful of crewmates at Rosemary's this morning. When he changed his plans, he got several curious looks for canceling. "Something came up, and I need to get home," he told them.

"I hope everything's okay," Tony said as Rob separated from the group and headed toward the parking area reserved for the crew. "If you need anything, let us know."

"I will. Thanks." He waved his hand behind him and headed for the Subaru.

At home, he dumped his dirty clothes into the laundry basket, changed the bedsheets just in case, and tidied up. He collected assorted magazines strewn across the coffee table and stacked them in a pile. Started a pot of coffee and set the table for two. He wasn't sure if Jenny had eaten at her place or if she planned to have breakfast with him. Despite the hunger gnawing his belly, he decided to wait and find out. He got out the eggs, bacon, toast, and jam. While he waited, he sat down at the table with his steaming mug and opened the mail, tossing most of it in the trash.

He was whipping up enough eggs for two when he heard Jenny's car pull up. As she neared the front door, Alcatraz woofed nice and loud. "Come on in," he greeted them both, then gave his dog a head rub and warm words of welcome. By then, Jenny had hung her coat in the closet. In a pair of jeans that hugged her curves and a pullover sweater, she looked good enough to eat. "I like that sweater," he said, fighting the urge to tug it over her head and feast on every inch of her body. He'd bet money she wanted that, but with Jenny, he never knew. "Have you had breakfast?"

"No, and don't let Alcatraz fool you with that pleading look. He's been fed and done his business."

Rob wasn't surprised. She always took care of the dog's needs first thing in the morning. He grinned at his canine. "You can't put anything past Jenny." Knowing he'd been found out, Alcatraz wandered into the living room, no doubt to chill on his doggie bed in the corner.

Her attention was on the bowl with the eggs and the plate of bacon strips waiting for the microwave. "What are you making?"

"A repeat of breakfast the other day, only the eggs will be scrambled. There's plenty for both of us."

He fixed her a cup of coffee and like the other day, invited her to help cook. They washed up and set to work, neither saying much until they sat down to eat. "Anything new since we last talked?" he asked, expecting a continuation of the discussion the other night. He wasn't about to push the conversation. That was up to her. "Did Hudson call Maddie?"

"Yesterday, after school. She said he apologized and seemed to mean it. That's what we hoped for."

Rob frowned. "Tell me he doesn't want to get back together."

"I don't think we have to worry about that. To quote Maddie, 'he's on my bad list.'"

"That's a relief." Jenny seemed uptight. "You okay?"

She sighed and set her fork down. "About our phone call the other night ..." Not quite meeting his gaze, she paused and her face flushed.

Yep, she wanted to talk sex, but the way she was acting, he couldn't decipher which way she wanted to go. His body went on full alert. Somehow, he maintained a neutral expression. "What are your thoughts?"

"I've decided—I mean—um—"

She was so nervous, it was painful to watch. "Put me out of my misery, Jenny, and spit it out. If you don't want sex, I'll live." Even if it killed him. He almost laughed at the thought.

"I want to set a few parameters, Rob. We agree that this has nothing to do with falling in love or getting serious."

"I'm with you on that. I've had my fill of serious relationships. God knows, I'm lousy at love and worse at marriage."

"We were pretty good at the love part, but we both bungled the marriage. For ages, I've been fine with singlehood, but someday I'd like to get married again. The girls are growing up and won't be living with either of us for more than another few years. I want a partner I can lean on when things get tough, a man who can lean on me, too. Someone to grow old with."

He hadn't known she wanted another marriage.

Didn't like the idea, and for sure didn't want to think about it. "Got it. Anything else?"

"A few more things. If for some reason one of us starts feeling serious, we agree to back away from what we started. No blame, no regrets. It goes without saying that what happens is between us and no one else." She bit her lip, which meant either she was holding something back, nervous, or both. Sucking in a breath, he waited to find out. "To be honest," she said, "Alicia might know something about this."

He stared at her. "You're saying you want to have sex, and Alicia knew before I did?"

"That's right. I apologize for discussing this with her first. I needed to run my decision by someone I trust, excluding my friends from the firehouse. Can you imagine what would happen if one of them let something slip to her partner? It'd spread all over. I wouldn't care about that if it weren't for Britt and Maddie. They can't know anything about this."

On board with everything she'd said, he nodded. "All good with me."

"Great. Anyway, Alicia will keep it to herself. I do the same when she confides in me." She paused. "I never imagined wanting to make love with you again, but lately it's all I think about. For the sake of my sanity, I *have* to be with you. Are you with me?"

"In every way." He reached across the little table and caught hold of her hands. "I want you, too. So much."

Still clutching his hand, she stood and pulled him up with her. "I'm on the pill."

"Good to know. I have condoms."

"Also good to know, but we don't need them. Let's go to bed."

~

JENNY HAD NEVER BEEN in Rob's bedroom, hadn't wanted to. She caught a glimpse of a king-size bed and reading tables on each side before he tugged her in for a kiss, and she forgot all about the décor. He wrapped his strong arms around her and brushed his lips over hers. A tease that wasn't enough, and she tugged him closer and kissed him with passion.

"You taste good," he murmured against her mouth, then kissed her again.

"From the breakfast and coffee." Already aching for more, she hooked her knee around the backs of his thighs.

"What you do to me," he groaned, grasping her bottom in his big hands and anchoring her as close as two fully clothed people could get.

"Show me," she replied, breathless.

He cupped her breasts, but her sweater and bra were in the way. Frustrated and needy, she stepped back to take them both off. When she was naked above the waist, he gazed at her, his big brown eyes shooting sparks her way. "You're as beautiful as I remember."

"Then your memory is faulty. My breasts aren't as perky as they used to be."

"They're perfect." He leaned in and nuzzled her, igniting her entire body. Soon his hands got in on the act, his fingers teasing her nipples the way she'd always liked. She nearly swooned. "I misspoke about your memory. You still know how to drive me wild."

"I remember everything you liked. Give me time and I'll prove it."

"You're not the only one with the great memory." Feeling bold, she undid the button at the top of his fly and slid the zipper down the bulge caused by his arousal. "I can't touch you the way I want, not with all those clothes on."

"You don't have to say that twice."

Scant minutes later, both naked, she feasted on the sheer perfection of the man. Fit, muscled, and fully erect, he was as gorgeous as ever. Better, even. He looked at her, too, with a reverent expression that made her feel special and desired. They reached for each other and tumbled onto the bed.

His hands and mouth were all over her, sending her straight toward a climax. His palms slid lower, to the most sensitive place. "You're already wet."

"I have been since I got here. That's how much I want this. Right now, please." She opened her thighs.

With a moan of pleasure, he entered her. She climaxed immediately—they both did—and the world trembled and broke into fragments that shimmered through her. When it was over, spent and sated, she clung to him. "That was amazing—you're amazing."

"Mind-blowing," he agreed, cradling her hip in his warm palm. "Equal to or better than the last time we had sex all those years ago."

"More than I ever imagined it could be. I can't believe we waited so long to do this."

"We haven't gotten along that well until recently." He brushed the hair back from her face and planted a tender kiss on her lips before sitting up. "I'll be right back."

He padded out of the room and stepped into the bathroom. While he was gone, she lay in his bed, her body humming and sated, her mind at peace. They'd been so connected, so in harmony, so united, it almost felt like love. *It isn't*, she assured herself. When it came to making love, they'd always been in sync. That's what made the sex so amazing. What she felt was lust, plain and simple. She'd never fall for him again, refused to let that happen. But the fact that she'd had the thought scared her.

Maybe they should stop now, avoid having sex again. She'd tell him as soon as he returned from the bathroom. A few minutes later and still gloriously naked, he entered carrying a warm cloth. "Thought you might need this." Alcatraz followed, his tail wagging. "Sorry, pal, you can't stay in here with us. We'll see you later." He escorted the canine out and closed the door.

He'd barely rejoined her in bed before the collie started in with high-pitched whining.

"Poor boy," Jenny said.

"Don't fall for the sad act. As you said, he's been fed and watered and done his business. He's playing us." Rob's eyes twinkled.

They both laughed, which led to a tickle fest and more laughter. Then kissing and other things that set her on fire all over again. She forgot all about what she'd wanted to say.

When she left a few hours later, she was torn between a repeat in the near future and stopping altogether. Regardless of what happened, she and Rob needed to talk.

21

For the rest of the day, including while he detailed a Rivian and throughout much of the night, Rob replayed the incredible morning with Jenny. Having sex in his bed multiple times had been unforgettable and had gotten better with practice. He couldn't wait to get together again. They were mature adults now, unafraid to teach each other new things they liked and wanted. Able to laugh, too. He'd really enjoyed that and hoped what they were sharing continued for a while. As long as the girls didn't find out. They wouldn't. No one else would, either, if he could help it. Alicia had better keep her mouth shut. But Jenny trusted her, and he had no choice but to do the same.

He held off contacting her again until the following afternoon. "I just finished a job on a gold Range Rover that cost about a hundred thousand but looked like it hadn't been cleaned since the guy bought it two years ago."

"Wow, that's a long time. With a car that pricey, you'd think the owner would take better care of it."

"Exactly what I assumed when I scheduled the

appointment. Took me hours more than I expected and looks great now."

"I hope he paid you well."

"He did and didn't complain when I charged him extra for the added time I spent. I also talked him into hiring me again in six months."

"I'm impressed. You really know how to sell."

"After all these years, I'd better." He stretched. "Anyway, I showered and put on clean clothes, and I feel good." He lowered his voice. "Wanna come over?"

"I can't, Rob. The girls will be home in about two hours."

"Too close to the end of the school day," he realized, wishing he'd been able to see her earlier.

"Don't sound so sad. I forgot to mention that the entire sophomore class is going on a field trip tomorrow."

"Almost two-hundred kids? Where are they going?"

"It's a riverboat trip to a wildlife refuge. They leave at nine a.m. and get back after dinner."

"Are they out of their minds? This is early November. It's cold outside."

"Apparently Orchard does this with the sophomores every November. According to them, the kids love it."

"I guess we'll find out." It also gave Jenny and him a long stretch of time to be alone, depending on her schedule. "Why don't we get together then?"

"Great idea. My house this time?"

"Sounds good. I don't have anything scheduled all day. I'll come in the morning."

"I'd rather wait till Alicia leaves around eleven. I think we should talk, too."

He didn't like the sound of that. What if she

wanted more out of the deal than what they'd agreed to? "We're talking now, so tell me."

"I will when you come over. I need to get to the store and pick up snacks for the field trip. See you tomorrow."

The rest of the day and evening stretched ahead of him. He scheduled several detailing jobs for the following week, ran around Guff's Lake with Alcatraz, dropped his dog off at home and fed him. For dinner, he took himself to The Rogue, a restaurant similar to Denny's only better, where he stuffed his face and wondered what Jenny wanted to discuss.

He slept in Friday morning, hung out with Alcatraz, then picked up treats for Jenny and him. Shortly after eleven, dreading whatever she wanted to say and resigned to listening, he pulled into her driveway.

~

JENNY WAS MAKING coffee when she heard Rob thud up the steps to the front porch. Crazy how eager she was to see him, when she wasn't sure how the conversation would play out. For all she knew, what she had to say could end what they'd both enjoyed right here. "Hi," she said and ushered him in. "Alicia left about ten minutes ago."

"Perfect timing. Since we're alone ..." He set a bakery bag with a Rosemary's Breakfast Nook label on the entry table, shrugged out of his coat, and kissed her.

Her hunger for him was immediate, but she wouldn't give in until they talked. She pulled away and glanced at the bag. "What's in there?"

"Samantha's cinnamon rolls."

Sam was Adam's fiancée and a wonderful baker

getting ready to open her own bakery. Meanwhile, she delivered her fresh, handmade baked goods daily to Rosemary's and several B&Bs in the area.

"Be still my heart." Jenny eyed the bag. "Looks like you have quite a few in there."

"They had a special buy one, get one free, so I bought extras for you, me, and some for the girls."

Such a nice guy. "They'll love it. But if I tell them you brought them over, they could get ideas about us."

"Not if you mention the special. They know I'm a sucker for good deals." He grabbed his jacket off the floor and hung it in the closet.

"That makes sense. How did you know I woke up this morning wishing I had a cinnamon roll?"

"I'm pretty familiar with your weaknesses," he said, then nuzzled the sensitive place below her ear before kissing her again.

Her entire body reacted, desire humming through her. "Don't," she said, fighting the urge to tug him closer. "Not until we talk."

Instantly, he stepped back. "Can we at least do that over coffee and a cinnamon roll?"

She wasn't in the mood to eat anything right now. "Yes on the coffee, but I'll save my treat for later. Let's sit in the kitchen."

They got their mugs and headed for the table. She waited till he sat down, then picked the seat across from him. Her table was round and roomier than his, and the choice of that particular seat seemed somehow safer. Never mind they'd sat across from each other a few days earlier and had ended up in bed together.

"What's on your mind?" he said tasting his coffee.

Ready to lay it out but at the same time nervous

for no reason at all, she cleared her throat. "You know how much I liked what we did."

"Me, too."

He looked at her with such desire, she almost forgot about what she wanted to say. Her heart expanded with the feelings that worried her. She brushed imaginary crumbs off the table, then told him point blank. "I don't want us to fall in love, and when you look at me that way ..." She let the rest hang there.

"So that's what's bothering you." Rob cupped his hands around the mug. "What you see when I look at you is the woman I've been lusting after nonstop—that's it. Oh, and I like you, too. *Like*," he repeated, studying her. "No love, just a strong attraction and a mutual affection for each other. Feeling better now?"

Not quite. "Since the divorce, we've both been involved with other people." Needing him to understand where she was coming from, she went on. "I don't know about you, but for me, none of the intimacy in my previous relationships comes close to what we shared the other day. I'm not sure if it means we happen to be extremely well-matched sexually, or if our feelings are stronger than we realize. I can't bear to think about what would happen then." There, she'd said it. "That's what scares me."

"Are you in love with me?" he asked with a guarded expression.

"No." She meant it.

"Then we're good. We talked about this Wednesday, remember?"

"Yes, but that was before we spent a lot of time in bed."

"When the sex is as amazing as ours, I see what we did as a necessity."

She couldn't argue with that. Once had definitely not been enough.

"I say let's enjoy this while it lasts," he said. "We done?"

"Not quite. People change and so could our feelings. What happens then?"

Her face must've shown her fear. Comprehension dawned on his face. "You don't want to have sex again, am I right?"

"Oh, I want to. But I think we should pull back."

He let out a dejected breath. "I can't say I'm happy about that, but if it's what you want ..."

Her brain said yes, but her body disagreed. Before she knew what was happening, she blurted out, "One more time can't hurt. Then we'll stop."

"Are you sure about this?"

"Mmm-hmm," she said and they headed upstairs.

22

Not counting Rob's days at the firehouse, he and Jenny found time to be together almost every day over the following two weeks, mostly at her house after Alicia left. Despite the discussion they'd had about giving up sex, neither of them wanted to. The more they made love, the more he wanted her, the way an addict might crave a drug. Lucky for him, Jenny seemed equally enthusiastic.

Friday morning, he was giving a client's minivan one last buff when she texted.

The twins are invited to a sleepover tonight. I'll come to your house after I drop them off.

He liked that. With the girls gone until the following day, she wouldn't have to rush home. Maybe she'd stay the night. The possibility wowed him. He texted a grinning emoji. *May as well bring an overnight bag.*

I can't wait. Will text when I'm on the way.

For the rest of the day, he thought about the night ahead. He wanted to take her out for dinner, but not with the possibility of someone seeing them together. The gossip was sure to follow and the if the girls heard something about it put a damper on that

... Not a problem—they'd order takeout to eat at home.

Chicken D-Lite tonight? He texted.

Yum.

When she let him know she was on her way, he phoned in an order, then got out two wine glasses for the chardonnay chilling in the fridge. The food arrived minutes before she did.

"Hi," she said, breezing in and bringing a gust of fresh air with her. "It's cold out there, and I'm freezing."

"Let's fix that." He set her small suitcase aside, hung her coat in the closet, and kissed her.

"Mmm," she said and kissed him back. "I'm already warmer."

"I can tell." He brushed her hair back and smiled. "I've been looking forward to this since you texted."

"Me, too." She sniffed the air. "Nothing better than the smell of piping hot food when I'm starving. I brought brownies."

"Good. Before I forget, I'm going to my folks' for brunch tomorrow."

"What time?"

"Ten-thirty. We'll be able to sleep in."

"I pick up the girls at ten, so that works out really well. You haven't seen your mom and dad in a while. That'll be fun. I'd ask you to tell them hello, but that might lead to questions you don't want to answer."

He agreed. They enjoyed a leisurely meal, chatting about work, the twins—they both had new boyfriends—and other everyday things. Too full for dessert, they decided to save it for later and settled in to stream a movie. That didn't last long before they ended up making out on the couch. Too turned on to make it to the bedroom, they had sex on the rug. Alcatraz, having been shut in the laundry room, whined piteously.

"Poor pooch. I'll let you out." Jenny threw on the robe she pulled out of her overnight bag which she'd conveniently left nearby, a short thing that showed off her very fine legs. She let him out while Rob stepped into his boxers and pulled his shirt on. To make up for penning him in, they gave him lots of love and a doggie treat.

In the kitchen, they topped the brownies with ice cream and spent a while eating and laughing and occasionally feeding each other. They were getting along better than he could ever remember, and decided to turn in early. First, they enjoyed a shower together. In bed, after talking and laughing, they enjoyed more sex.

He fell asleep sated and happy with her in his arms.

JENNY WOKE up in the dark of night feeling warm and content, although she wasn't sure where she was. She turned her head, caught the heady whiff of masculine male that was uniquely Rob mixed with the scent of sex, and remembered. She was in his bed. Smiling, she glanced at the clock. Three a.m., plenty of time to fall asleep again. She was on the verge of doing exactly that when she realized something was different. *She* was different. At some point, without realizing it, her feelings for Rob had deepened.

The worst had happened. She loved him.

Terrified of what it meant and the repercussions sure to follow, she pulled out of his arms. He didn't so much as stir. Her suitcase was near the bedroom door where she'd brought it, yesterday's clothes in the small laundry bag inside. She needed another shower, but that could wait until she was home. By feel, she found the change of clothes and dressed.

Then she returned to the bed and stood beside the slumbering man she loved. "Rob," she said, hating to disturb him.

He jerked awake. "Yeah?"

"I have to go home."

"What time is it?" He started to sit up.

"Three a.m. Go back to sleep."

To her relief, he did. Just now, she had too much on her mind to talk about her feelings.

At home, she was too upset to rest. Standing under a hot shower, she scolded herself. Hadn't she worried about this from the beginning? Why hadn't she followed her instincts after the first time they'd had sex and put an end to it right there? Rob would've been okay with that.

Because she'd wanted him too much to stop what they'd started. He was the same way. The agreement that love wouldn't play into their relationship had reassured them to go full bore with the lovemaking.

And now, want to or not, she'd broken the agreement and lost her heart to him. She wasn't sure how he felt but had a fair idea her feelings weren't reciprocated. Which was good—he didn't want her love any more than she wanted to love him.

In hindsight, the agreement seemed ridiculous, an excuse for having sex without worrying about the inevitable fallout. The time to pay the consequences for that had come, putting an end to the loving and intimacy between them. No more seeing each other except to pick up or drop off the twins.

Her entire being protested, but so be it. "I'm such

an idiot," she groaned as she stared at herself in the bathroom mirror and dressed for the day ahead. Hating the hangdog look on her face, she straightened her spine and held her head up high—for all the good that did. "I have to tell him," she promised, although the thought pierced her heart like an arrow.

But when? Not this morning. She had to pick up the girls, and he was at brunch with his parents. She wasn't sure how to work such a conversation into the day, but it had to be soon.

Not tonight, either, when he brought Alcatraz over around dinnertime and the girls were home. Best to act friendly but not overly so, the same as always when their daughters were around, and let him know she had something to tell him. That'd work. For the rest of the day, her stomach was tied in knots.

23

R ob woke up Sunday morning in a great mood. After the fantastic night he'd spent with Jenny, how could he not be? Had she really left at three a.m.? What a shame, when she could've stayed longer. Whistling, he fed Alcatraz, then let him out into the fenced back yard. After showering and dressing, he called the dog in. "Gonna see my parents," he said. "Be good. We'll go out running when I get back."

He stopped at Rosemary's before driving to their house and arrived with a box of croissants still warm from the bakery. They still lived in the ranch-style home they'd bought when he was a baby. The door was unlocked and he let himself in. They greeted him warmly, both beaming at him.

His mother, a good five inches shorter than he was, hugged him. "It's good to see you."

His father, exactly his height, patted his shoulder. They hadn't been close during his childhood, but over the years their relationship had grown warmer. "You look happy. How are you?"

"Happy" didn't begin to describe Rob's euphoric

mood. "I'm great. Glad to be here. Brought croissants from Rosemary's."

"Thanks from the bottom of my heart," his mother said with delight. "We'll have them with breakfast."

Rob sniffed the air. "Sure smells good in here."

"I made a brunch casserole with a recipe from the paper. Let's eat."

They sat down at the kitchen table and dug in. As always, the conversation centered on him and the twins. Like Jenny, he was an only child.

"How are the girls?" his mom wanted to know. "The last I heard was when you called to tell us Maddie passed that test."

"A relief for all of us. A lot has happened since then." He filled them in about the Halloween disaster, assuring them she was okay now and seemed to be doing well. "Britt loves school, especially World Lit and science. That's new."

"Maybe she'll be a scientist or a college professor someday," his dad said.

"Could be, although she might be into something else soon. She's at that age. Both girls are looking forward to seeing you on Thanksgiving. They were both at a sleepover last night. I doubt they slept much."

Thanks to Jenny, neither had he.

"They'll be tired tonight," his mom said.

His dad chuckled. "They're kids, they'll bounce back soon. How's the mother of my grandchildren?" he asked as the meal wound down. Rob's parents liked Jenny and often asked about her.

"Fine." Excellent. Amazing. "She's busy with work and the girls."

They nodded. "You're getting along?" his mother asked.

Lately, almost always. Especially in bed. Even

thinking about that blew his mind. "Pretty much," he said, playing it cool. "It's better for the girls."

As he headed home, he thought about Jenny and wanted her again. Sex with her was magical. Too bad they couldn't spend another night together. With the girls home today, that was impossible. A shame she'd left his bed in the middle of the night. Odd, too. She must've had her reasons.

Eventually, he figured out a possible one—spending a full night together had felt too serious. The thought resonated with him, too, which got him thinking. From now on, it'd be best to skip overnights.

They'd talk about that later. If not tonight, the next time they were alone.

THE SLEEPOVER RAN LATE, and Jenny picked the twins up shortly after eleven. They hadn't had much sleep and weren't in the best moods. She was tired, too, but at least they didn't notice her equally sour attitude. Leaving them at home with their petty arguments, she headed for the grocery and stocked up for the coming week, including Thanksgiving. She spent part of the afternoon outside, pruning here and there, raking leaves and cleaning out the kennels for the following morning. Normally she'd have made the girls help her, but she wanted to be alone and they seemed fine with that.

So nice to be outdoors in the crisp air with her mind on her chores. Inside again later, she did the laundry. She was working on dinner when Alcatraz woofed and Rob knocked at the door. Not ready to face him, she asked Britt to let him in while she got the meatloaf ready to bake.

The girls greeted their dad and the dog with hugs. "How was the sleepover?" he asked.

"Good," Maddie said.

Britt nodded. "It was so fun. We had lots of stuff to eat and shows to stream."

Afraid to look at Rob—he might notice something had changed—Jenny kept her head down as she peeled potatoes. "They didn't get much sleep and have been grouchy all day," she said.

The twins glanced at each other. "Sorry, Mom," Britt said. "I should've taken a nap."

Maddie yawned. "We're going to bed early."

"That's a good idea. Don't forget to thank your father for the cinnamon rolls he dropped off last week," she reminded them.

"Thanks, Dad," Maddie said.

"They were delicious," Britt added. "And it was nice of you to bring them over. Feel free to do it again any time."

"Okay." He chuckled.

Jenny basted the potatoes with butter, then slid them and the meatloaf into the oven. When she finished, Rob was studying her. "You seem tired, too," he commented without a trace of irony. When he knew she'd been up at three a.m.

"I am."

He didn't seem tired or anything out of the ordinary, which for some reason irritated her, even though he had no idea how much things had changed. She chalked that up to fatigue.

All of a sudden, now seemed the right time to tell him she didn't want to have sex anymore or anything else except where the girls were involved. Her heart constricted at the thought, but she had to move past that and him. She set the peeler down and wiped her hands on a towel. "I need to talk to your dad." By the girls' wide eyes, they wanted to hear all about it. As if. "Alone. Please go upstairs. I'll call you when dinner's ready."

As soon as their footsteps faded away, signaling they were up there, she gestured for him to sit down at the table. He was quiet and somber, as if he somehow sensed the seriousness of the conversation they were about to have. Anxious to shed the weight she'd carried since she'd left his bed, she swallowed and let it out. "I can't go on like this, Rob."

She heard the door to their room close and realized they'd been listening. At least, they hadn't heard much. She put her finger to her mouth. "Did you hear the door click when it closed just now?" she said, her voice barely above a whisper. "They were eavesdropping."

"Stinkers," he quipped in an equally low voice." Sharing a *what-can-you-do* look with her, he almost grinned. Then quickly sobered. "I get it—spending a whole night together makes things feel way more serious than either of us wants, even if it wasn't the entire night. We don't have to do that again."

If that wasn't verification his feelings weren't as strong as hers ... She ought to be relieved. Instead, she was a total wreck. Why had she fallen for him? Time to tell him the relationship had to end. After blowing out a heavy breath, she plunged ahead. "I agree, things have gotten way too intense between us. That's why I think it's time we stop what we've been doing." The words tore her apart, and she felt sick inside.

Clearly taken aback, Rob scrubbed his hand over his face like he did when something unexpected and not to his liking happened. "This comes out of the blue." He was quiet a moment, then, "Are you saying you lo—"

Dreading the question that was coming and not about to answer it, she raised her hand, palm out, and silenced him. "No regrets, no questions, no blame, remember? We go back to seeing and contacting each other when it involves the girls, the way it's been since we divorced, only without the fighting."

"I'm not sure I follow. Everything was great last night, now it's not? Can we talk about this?"

Break down in front of him? She shook her head. "I'd rather not."

His expression blanked. "I guess I shouldn't be surprised. When things got rough during our marriage, you never wanted to talk them through."

True, but he was equally at fault. She sighed. "Neither of us did. Instead of solving our problems, we had sex, and that's no way to fix things." Any second now, she'd fall apart. She didn't want him to see that, wanted him gone. "I'm sure the girls are wondering what we're talking about. They expect me to be open about my relationships, but they don't know a thing about us and I'm not going to tell them."

"We agreed on that. Let's stick with the decision. I assume you'll go ahead with Thanksgiving day as planned?"

"Of course. My dad and Adelle are looking forward to it, and I'm sure your parents are, too. Help me out, Rob. What do I tell our daughters?"

"If we're friendly and act like nothing has changed, they'll be fine."

"I doubt pretending all is well will be enough. No matter what either of us says or have said, the expectation that we're getting back together is all over their faces." At the thought of their dashed hopes, tears gathered behind her eyes. While she still had a semblance of control, she stood. "Dinner's almost ready, and you need to go home and prep for your shift."

"Right." He pushed to his feet and donned his coat. "Good luck with the girls and have a decent week."

Jenny didn't think that was possible. "Do you want to say goodbye to them?"

"Not tonight. I'll see them in four days, when I pick them up for Thanksgiving dinner at my folks'. Tell them I said to sleep well."

Then he was gone.

24

While their parents talked in the kitchen, Maddie and Britt holed up in their room. Both upset, they talked about what little they'd heard. "I can't believe what Mom said to Dad," Maddie huffed. "She doesn't want to be nice to him anymore? I hate her for that!"

"It's awful," Britt agreed. "What was she thinking? I hated it when they were tense all the time. Now they'll start that again." She mimed sticking her finger down her throat. "I don't want to see or talk to her tonight or anytime soon."

"Then let's not." That'd show her. Except, even through the closed door, Maddie smelled dinner cooking. "She made meatloaf and those yummy crispy potatoes. We could wait until she's asleep and then go downstairs and eat, but I'm hungry now."

"I'm too tired to wait up, anyway," Britt said. "I don't want to sit at the table with Mom, but I want to find out why she did that. She's not supposed to keep secrets anymore, and we deserve to know."

Maddie nodded. "Let's ask her to tell us. If she won't, we'll keep on her until she does."

They waited till she called them to dinner, then

slunk down the stairs. One look at her mom's face, and Maddie forgot about the plan to find out why she'd been so mean to their dad. Her eyes were red like she'd been crying, and her bottom lip looked like she'd chewed on it a lot. Their mom never cried. What'd happened?

"Are you okay, Mom?" Britt asked, looking every bit as puzzled as Maddie.

"Yes, just exhausted. I think I'll go to bed early. You two go ahead and eat. Be sure to wash up first. When you finish, clean up your mess and put the leftovers in the fridge."

Not about to let her leave without talking at least a little, Maddie fiddled with her hair. "Dad didn't say goodnight to us."

"He said to wish you a good sleep."

Maddie and her sister looked at each other. That wasn't at all like him. Unable to contain her curiosity any longer, she asked the question on her mind. "What's going on with you guys? Why did you tell him you couldn't be nice to him anymore?"

Their mom frowned as if thinking about it. "That's right, you eavesdropped at first. That's not quite what I said—the word 'nice' never came up." Her heavy sigh was filled with gloom, and her eyes looked watery.

"Well, what did you say?" Britt asked.

"I—I'm way too tired to talk about anything right now."

"But you promised not to keep secrets."

"I know. I'm going to bed."

Without any dinner? Forget making her explain herself. Maddie gaped at her. "You have to eat, Mom. That's what you always tell us."

"I'm so tired, I'm nauseated. Don't worry, I'll eat a hearty breakfast in the morning. Goodnight."

As she trudged up the stairs to her bedroom, Britt let out a concerned sigh. "I've never seen her like this. Maybe she's getting sick."

"If she was, she'd have told us. This has something to do with Dad."

They sat down to the meal. Maddie had lost her appetite but the food tasted so good, she managed to eat. So did her sister. During the meal, they continued talking. "She should've told us what we heard wrong when she said stuff to Dad. Then he leaves without a goodbye? He's never done that before. He must be messed up, too."

Britt bit her lip. "I wish we knew what happened, but we don't know how to find out. Let's clean up and go to bed."

Later, as Maddie and her sister laid out their clothes for school the following day and got ready for bed, the conversation about their parents resumed. "Mom's probably asleep," she said. "I wonder how Dad's doing? I think we should call him. Maybe he'll tell us what's going on."

"I doubt he'll explain, either. He's as secretive as she is." Britt checked her phone for the time. "It's not that late, but he might've turned in early like Mom did."

Maddie hadn't considered that. "Let's text him good night instead and save our questions for another time."

Britt frowned. "You want to send one text from both of us?"

"Why not?"

They composed the message together and both signed it. Their dad didn't reply. As they'd assumed, he was already asleep. Shortly after that, they followed suit.

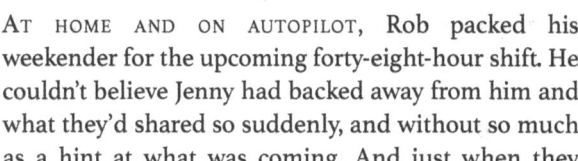

AT HOME AND ON AUTOPILOT, Rob packed his weekender for the upcoming forty-eight-hour shift. He couldn't believe Jenny had backed away from him and what they'd shared so suddenly, and without so much as a hint at what was coming. And just when they were getting along so well.

He felt numb and couldn't quite make sense of it. She'd said things had gotten too intense, and he'd agreed. If she wanted to go back to where they'd been —minus the tension—either she was on the verge of falling for him or worried she would. Maybe she was tired of the sex, but the way she participated and reciprocated, that seemed unlikely.

He'd tried to find out, but she'd shut him down, pretty much like when they'd been married. Plain and simple, he was clueless and had no idea what was in her head. Oh, man. He scratched the back of his neck. No point trying to guess what she wasn't saying. It was what it was—over. Or so he figured. There was no way to know for sure. Tired of thinking about it, he shut his devices off and went to bed. Sleep didn't come easily. When it finally did, the alarm woke him way earlier than he wanted. Deprived of his rest and in a foul mood, he was in no way ready to face the team or anyone else.

After showering and dressing, which helped him wake up, he turned his devices back on and found a text from Britt and Maddie. *Hi, Dad. We didn't get to say goodnight to u. R u mad at me & her? Please don't be. Have a good day tomorrow, Maddie & Britt.*

Double damn. His daughters had texted him. He sent a short message. *I'm not mad at you. Will be in touch when I can. Love you both.*

At the firehouse, he stowed his stuff, then went to the kitchen to eat the sausage roll he'd bought. Most of the guys were there, breakfasting and catching up on what they'd done over the weekend. Daniel nodded. "Hey."

Rob grumbled a greeting and got a bunch of sideways looks.

"What's wrong with you?" Gus said.

He didn't plan to say anything but did anyway. "Jenny, that's what."

"Don't tell me you're having problems with each other again?"

The kitchen filled with collective groans and guys talking all at once.

Waiting for the noise to die down, he thought about what to say. May as well tell them about her and him now that it was in the past.

"Since there's no reason to hide anything ... This is for your ears only—we don't want the twins finding out. We've been seeing each other." He scrubbed his hand through his hair. "Now we're not."

"Nothing new about you two getting together," Liam said. "Everyone at the firehouse knows, wives and girlfriends included."

Rob gaped at the man. "That's not possible. What clued you in?" As soon as he asked, he figured it out. "The night of the Halloween party."

"That was the beginning. You both disappeared for a while. And then ... Let's just say, you were seen going to her place in the morning after the twins caught their bus to school."

Mystified, he scowled. "What the hell? You spied on us?"

"No way. Some of us board our dogs at Jenny's place, remember?"

"So what?"

"We've seen your car parked in the driveway or nearby. It wasn't hard to put two and two together."

"Wow. Can't put anything past you guys. FYI, I was there to pick up Alcatraz like I do every Wednesday morning."

"Yeah, but your car was there for a long time, and not just Wednesdays."

"So you *have* been spying. Is nothing sacred?" Rob shook his head. "We've also been talking about Britt and Maddie."

"Sure that's all you're doing?" Liam asked.

"Were doing," Rob corrected. "We're not anymore."

"So things between you, Jenny, and the girls were good, but now they're not."

Unable to lie, he shrugged. "Things are still good with the twins."

Daniel eyed him. "I thought we were close. I took on some of your morning appointments. I figured you'd talk to me about her, but you didn't."

"I never said anything to anybody till a few minutes ago. You sure as hell didn't let on you knew anything." Rob glanced around the room. "None of you did." That stung. "What's with you guys?"

"We figured you'd talk about it in your own time."

Some answer that was.

"And now you and Jenny aren't together?" Daniel cocked his head. "What happened?"

"Beats me. All I know is, she's not into me anymore."

"She pulled the plug?" Liam frowned. "That's harsh."

· · ·

"Don't tell me she's seeing another man," Tony said.

Rob hadn't thought of that last night. Surely she wouldn't make love with so much feeling and passion if she were seeing someone besides him. Hating the idea, he curled his lip. "She'd better not be doing that."

"Couples have misunderstandings all the time," Liam commented, "especially you two. Are you sure she meant to call it quits?"

"I was there—I should know," he growled.

Seemingly unflappable, Gus eyed him. "Sounds to me like you have strong feelings for her. Real strong."

Dude had that right. Rob narrow-eyed him. "Can we stop talking about it now?"

"We won't say another word," Ethan said. "Your daughters won't hear anything from us."

"Or your significant others," Rob reminded them before he remembered. "Scratch that. They already know." He made sure to include each of them in his dirty look. Then, muttering a few choice words, he wrapped up his uneaten breakfast for later and stood. "I have work to do."

As soon as he left, Gus conferred with Owen. "I'm calling Wanda to update her. You contact Hallie. They ought to know."

"Don't tell Rob. He might not like it."

"He doesn't have a choice. The damage is done."

25

That same Monday, Jenny woke up ahead of the alarm from a surprisingly good night's sleep. For a few moments, she felt great. Then the events of the previous evening flooded back. Feelings she'd never wanted to experience again—sorrow, and the empty feeling of losing something important—flooded back. Determined to be positive and make the day a good one, she shoved them away and focused on the morning ahead.

Before checking to ensure the girls were awake, she made coffee. While it perked, she stepped into the shower. Standing under the spray, she cried a little before she pulled herself together. As soon as she dressed, she woke the girls in plenty of time to eat breakfast and catch the bus, lying through her teeth with assurances that she felt better now that she was rested. When in truth, she wanted to roll up into a ball and sob her heart out.

As soon as she sent them on their way, she drained her mug, then headed outside to take care of her boarders. "This is going to be a great day," she told the dogs and assured herself. That done, she tromped inside again. Although she wasn't hungry, she made herself the go-to breakfast she'd turned to as a child when she'd disappointed her mother for some reason or other and had had to rely on her own cooking skills. A peanut butter and jam sandwich on toast. "Yum," she said out loud, though not with much enthusiasm, while she ate it.

That done, she did something completely out of character and canceled the Monday morning meeting at the Fashion Dogs office. "I'm dealing with some personal things," she said by way of explanation. "We'll meet next Monday, after Thanksgiving. Have a wonderful holiday."

When Alicia arrived to walk the dogs, she fixed Jenny with a questioning look. "Something's wrong. Are you okay?"

Jenny shook her head. "I broke things off with Rob, but I don't want to talk about it now. I canceled my meeting this morning. After our walk, I'm going to put up my feet and escape into a suspense novel."

"Good idea. I'm sorry," Alicia said.

"Me, too. It hurts." Jenny changed the subject to the weather and other light topics.

When the dog walk ended and the boarded dogs were safely in their kennels, Alicia got ready to leave. "Enjoy your book. If you need to talk, I'm here."

"Thanks, I'll—" the phone rang. "It's Wanda," she said. What was she doing, calling when she was supposed to be working at the hair and nail salon she owned? "I have to take this call. I'll fill you in on everything later, when I don't feel so miserable."

As Alicia headed for her car, Jenny answered the call. "Good morning," she said, sounding blah to her own ears.

"Hi, sweetie. Hallie and I are coming over shortly, so stay put."

"What for?"

"We'll tell you when we get there."

By the time they showed up some half hour later, Jenny had pulled herself together and made a fresh pot of coffee. They brought a treat bag.

"What's all this for?" she asked. "You both skipped work, and brought treats? It's not my birthday."

"I own the salon, and I can go in late," Wanda said.

"And I happen to be between assignments," Hallie replied. "We brought assorted scones and muffins, and lots of chocolate." She rubbed her hands together.

Wanda pulled a platter from the cabinet, arranged the treats, and set them on the table.

Jenny was thoroughly confused. "I don't understand."

Both women gave her sympathetic looks. "We heard you broke up with Rob," Wanda said.

In the process of setting out plates, mugs, sugar, and half-and-half on the table, Jenny's jaw dropped. No one knew they'd been seeing each other. Unless ... Surely Rob hadn't told anyone, especially not her girlfriends. "Help me out here and explain."

This time, Hallie did the talking. "At the firehouse, it's common knowledge that you two got back together weeks ago."

"I wouldn't go that far," Jenny corrected them. "We were seeing each other, though. Rob and I agreed to keep what we were doing to ourselves because we didn't want the girls to know. How did you find out?"

"We all knew you two were sleeping together."

There went Jenny's mouth again, gaping in horror. She groaned. "Do I want to know how you came to that conclusion?"

"With Rob parking at your house in the mornings after the girls left for school, it wasn't that hard to figure out," Wanda explained. Before Jenny could re-act, she went on. "We're your closest friends, and you didn't tell us."

Both women looked genuinely sad. Jenny felt terri-ble. "I love you guys and would've said something, only I couldn't. Rob and I thought we were the only two in the know. I guess I should explain. When we decided to get physical after all these years, we agreed not to get serious. We're so different and our track record together was pretty bad. We never said this to each other, but the assumption was that sooner or later our relationship would end. That's why we didn't tell anyone. We didn't want our girls finding out we were together only to get hurt when we weren't."

"What's this about you two breaking things off?" Wanda asked, scrutinizing her.

"You know about that, too?" Breakfast at the fire-house kitchen must've been a doozie.

"All I know is what Gus said when he called earlier —Rob was in a foul mood at breakfast because you broke up with him."

"He said that?" How could he, when they promised not to tell anyone? For a minute, anger al-most took the place of hurt. Almost, not quite. Appar-ently, Jenny could feel both at the same time. The tears she'd held back threatened to fall, even when she bit her lip and blinked them away. She swiped at her eyes furiously.

"I'm so sorry," Hallie murmured, her voice laced with sympathy. "Don't blame Rob, though. The guys already knew."

How had they known? What did it matter, any-way? She and Rob were no longer together. "I wouldn't call it breaking up, just taking a huge step back. I had to," she blubbered, full-on crying now.

Wanda's expression was filled with compassion. "Oh, sweetie."

Hallie patted her arm. "What exactly happened?"

Fishing in her pocket for a tissue, Jenny wiped her eyes and considered what to say. Her friends knew the general story, so there was no harm in sharing the details. "After the awful night at Harvey's, we agreed we had to get back on track and get along better than we used to."

Both women nodded and she continued. "I'm sure Gus and Owen told you about the massages we had. That was an experiment to see if relaxing would help ease the tension between us. Surprisingly, it did. We actually got along for several hours, and a funny thing happened. We realized we were attracted to each other after thirteen years apart. That came as a shock —sort of. I never stopped thinking he was sexy. Apparently, he felt the same about me. And, well, you know how it is when you can't resist each other."

"We know, all right," Hallie said. "Go on."

"We discovered we're still compatible in bed. He's a wonderful lover." The best Jenny had ever had. She paused to blow her nose. "Then I had to go and fall back in love with him and ruin everything."

Wanda squinted at her as if she'd lost her marbles. "Maybe I'm crazy, but I don't see a problem there."

The tears had dried up, a relief. "I guess I didn't explain that. Before we had sex, we agreed not to get serious. We're of different minds about what we want. I hope to get married again someday. Rob made it clear that after our disastrous marriage and a few other relationships that didn't work out, he wasn't looking to settle down anytime soon."

"From what Owen said, he sure is hurt."

"So am I. Anyway, we're not going to see each

other anymore except like before, when we have to for the girls."

Hallie frowned. "He was upset when you said you love him?"

"He doesn't know, and I'm not going to tell him." Jenny was sure he'd freak out.

"Because you think he doesn't have feelings for you?"

"Oh, he does. He likes me, but most of that is related to sex."

"Then why is he so bummed about the breakup?"

Jenny didn't even have to think about that. "You don't have to love someone to feel rotten. We had a good thing going, now we don't."

"You didn't ask, but here's my advice. Maddie and Britt are smart. The split between you and Rob won't go unnoticed by them. Plus, with the two of us and everyone at the station knowing what they do, word is bound to get out. You don't want the girls to find out about this from someone else. If it were me, in the very near future I'd tell them what's going on."

Something to discuss with Rob—if Jenny could approach him without falling apart. She'd promised the twins to be more open about her relationships and guessed she ought to follow through somehow, without going into details. If that was even possible. "That's a good idea."

After a three-way hug with her friends, she felt better. Not great, though. Want to or not, she needed to talk to Rob. Better contact him now, before the twins got home.

He didn't answer so she left a message. "It's me. I guess everyone at the firehouse knows about us. I think we should tell the girls, although I'm not sure what to say, before someone else does. We shouldn't wait too long. Call me."

So FAR, Monday at the firehouse was quiet. No calls, no alarms. Rob worked out, caught up on chores, and sat in on the monthly safety-training class in the training room. When it ended, he checked his phone and found a voice mail from Jenny. He was hurting pretty bad from what'd happened the previous night and wasn't sure he wanted to talk to her. When he heard what she had to say, he phoned her right away.

"Got your message," he said when she answered. "Before we talk, I need to explain about breakfast this morning. I never meant to say anything about us—it just slipped out. Not a one of them was surprised. They all knew we've been seeing each other, but no one bothered to mention it to me. Not even Daniel," he snarled, still steamed.

"I don't blame you for being upset. They're brothers to you and should've said something. I'm not thrilled, either, that people didn't let on what they knew. Wanda and Hallie stopped by earlier and en-lightened me. They heard about us breaking up and brought comfort treats."

"No way. What about your usual Monday morning Fashion Dogs meeting?"

"I called in sick."

"That's a new one for you."

"I know, but I wasn't up to it." Rob totally under-stood. "All this time, we thought we were being sneaky. What a joke." Neither of them spoke for a few moments before she went on. "Anyway, now that what happened is common knowledge, we have to tell the girls, and soon, before they find out from someone else. They deserve to hear it from us. We'll say we thought about getting together and changed our minds."

He approved of the idea. "That'll work. They texted last night, wanting to know if I was okay because I didn't wish them good night."

"Aww, so sweet. What'd you say?"

"I didn't reply till this morning. I texted that I was asleep when their message arrived and appreciated them thinking of me."

"Perfect. They texted you together? That's a first. Here's another—they were worried about me last night because I skipped dinner."

"It smelled so good, my mouth watered. How could you resist?"

To his surprise, Jenny laughed, but only for a moment before she got serious again. "Last night was sad. Also, I was too tired to eat. Don't worry, this morning I had breakfast, and a scone, and a muffin."

"Lucky you. I didn't eat today till I nuked a cold sausage roll midmorning."

"That doesn't sound too bad."

"You wouldn't say that if you tasted it." He was enjoying the back and forth, his pain blunted and lousy mood almost forgotten, when the truth hit him. At some unknown point, he'd fallen head over heels for his ex-wife. "I'll be damned, and not in a good way," he muttered.

"What did you say?"

"Nothing." And after they'd agreed that love had no place in their relationship. By getting involved with her, he'd taken a risk he never should've. Big mistake she didn't need to know about, unless she was in the same boat. But thanks to her refusal to explain her reason for breaking up with him, he had no idea and wasn't about to chance baring his soul.

"Rob? Are you there?"

"Still am."

"So, when do we tell our daughters?"

No way was he up to it now. He thought for a minute. "Thanksgiving is in three days. I vote for talking to them the following day—if you think we can wait that long."

"I'd rather wait forever, but we can't. Do we tell them together or apart?"

"I don't know, Jenny, I feel pretty raw." Really bad, like his gut had been ripped open. That's what he got for falling in love.

"I'm not so good, either, but we have to decide."

"Okay, then. Together."

26

Thanksgiving was one of Jenny's favorite holidays. The girls celebrated twice, two separate feasts—one midday and the other early evening. Every other year, she and Rob traded the times. This was her year for the earlier meal. Late afternoon, Rob would pick them up and take them to his parents' for the second one.

Despite her broken heart, she was determined to keep the day festive and fun. Pushing her sorrow away, she put on a happy face and pretended all was well. That helped, and she managed to fool Maddie and Britt. They loved the holiday and filled the house with their laughter and excitement, making it easy for Jenny to smile. They set the table and helped cook, baking the from-scratch pies and rolls themselves, while her dad and Adelle were bringing two side dishes. Jenny handled the rest.

Shortly before noon, her father and Adelle arrived with a bottle of wine in addition to the side dishes. Adelle was warm and friendly to the girls, and they seemed to take to her as well. Jenny surprised herself and ended up laughing for the first time in days and truly enjoying the whole thing.

Several hours later, full to the point of bursting, Adelle and her father left. The girls helped clear the table, then headed upstairs to pack—they'd stay at Rob's from tonight through the weekend. After bringing their suitcases downstairs, they set out for a walk to settle their stomachs before the next feast.

As soon as the door shut behind them, the joy she'd felt faded away. The house was too quiet. The thought of spending the long weekend alone brought her feelings dangerously close to the surface, but darn it, this was the wrong time for a pity party. She raised her head. "I'm going to have a great time all weekend," she promised herself aloud. "I'll find fun things to do —design cute new coats and sweaters for dogs, get together with friends, see a movie or two, and sleep till noon if I want." Make soups and casseroles from the leftovers as well to freeze for later. "So buck up, Jenny Carver!"

Talking to herself like she was someone else? She shook her head. But the pep self-talk helped.

She hoped it held.

∾

"WALKING OUTDOORS FEELS GOOD, even if it is cold," Maddie said as a chilly wind whipped the air.

"I'm glad we're out here," Britt agreed. "I'm not so full anymore. If I'm lucky, I'll be able to eat the turkey dinner at Grandma and Grandpa's."

"It's a good thing we won't sit down to eat till almost seven." Maddie shoved her gloved hands into her coat pockets. "It'll be dark before long. I hate that it happens so early around here, don't you? Dad should be at the house soon to pick us up. Let's go home."

They were a few blocks from the house when they saw Mrs. Taylor, a neighbor and widow some years younger than their grandparents, taking a walk with her son and his wife. Their cute baby, Mica, was strapped in a carrier on his mother's chest. Mica and his parents didn't live far from Mrs. Taylor, and she took care of him while they were at work.

"Happy Thanksgiving," Mrs. Taylor called out in a cheerful voice.

"Happy Thanksgiving to all of you," Britt and Maddie chimed together.

Mica's parents smiled. "Are you as full as we are?"

Britt patted her stomach through her parka. "We ate way too much, and we're going to our grandparents' in a little while to eat more. That's why we're out here walking."

"It's that time of the year." Mrs. Taylor looked so happy. "It seems like a long time since I've seen you girls. You've grown up so much."

Maddie was used to hearing that. "Can we see Mica?"

"Of course," his mom said, and gestured them over.

He cooed and smiled, and Maddie and her sister enjoyed making him giggle. "He's adorable," Britt said.

Then he got fussy. "It's naptime," his mom explained. "We should get him home."

The parents and baby left, but Mrs. Taylor lingered. She had more to say. "Before I forget—I saw your mom and dad last week. I was glad to see them together again. I know you must be, too."

Maddie was too stunned to reply, but Britt didn't seem to have that problem. "When did you see them?"

"The other day, right after your mother finished

walking the dogs. Your dad was getting out of his car and she was outside waiting."

In the morning? Maddie wondered about that. "He was probably picking up Alcatraz, and she decided to wait with him."

"I didn't see any sign of that sweet dog. Anyway, please wish them a Happy Thanksgiving from me. I'm going to hurry back to the house now and get warm."

"What was she talking about?" Britt said in a soft voice as they continued their walk toward home.

"I don't know, but she's wrong about our parents. They were probably getting along when she saw them, but after what mom said to dad the other night? They sure aren't now."

"Not at all—Mom hasn't even mentioned him." Britt looked thoughtful. "Mrs. Taylor must be mistaken. She couldn't have seen them together." She paused. "But what if she did?"

More secrets. Maddie's temper flared. "I knew they were keeping something from us, and after Mom promised to tell us stuff. They'd better explain what's going on, or else."

"That's right." Britt sounded mad, too. She pointed up the street. "Look, Dad's car is in the driveway."

"They'd better be straight with us."

"What if they won't?" Britt asked, as they drew closer to the house.

"We'll make them."

"How?"

"It has to be something big, like ..." Maddie thought a moment. "I'm not sure yet. We need time to figure that out. Let's walk around the block until we do."

∾

IN THE KITCHEN, Jenny put on the Beyoncé *Cowboy* album and decided to do the dishes. She was uncomfortably full, and moving around always helped. While the sink filled, she danced and sang along with the music, her thoughts on Rob. Any minute now, he'd be here. It'd been several days since they'd spoken. The thought of seeing him tonight, even for a little while, made her weak with love. But the short-lived romance between them was finished, and she needed to put it behind her and hide her feelings. That wouldn't be easy but had to be.

Tell him how you feel, a little voice in her head prompted. "I can't," she whispered aloud, because admitting it would make her look weak. She couldn't bear for him to see her in that light. Even the thought was mortifying. She turned up the volume and attempted to lose herself in the beat while she tackled the gravy pan.

She was scrubbing the thing furiously when she heard the knock at the door. She peered through the peephole. Rob was here. Fluttering and nervous, she lowered the volume of the music and let him in. "Hi," she said.

"Hey." His parka was unzipped, providing glimpses of his dress pants and pressed shirt. He looked so handsome. Her heart twinged painfully. They shared a long look while she fought to seem okay. With his carefully blank expression, she had no idea what he was thinking. "Happy Thanksgiving," she said to end the uncomfortable silence between them.

"You, too." He shifted from one foot to the other. "This is awkward," he commented, sliding his hands into his pants pockets.

"Times ten. The girls are out walking to make room for the turkey feast at your parents'."

"Good idea." His gaze roved from her head to her feet. "I like that dress—what I can see of it under the apron. You look beautiful."

"Thanks. So do you—handsome, I mean."

His compliment and the warmth in his eyes bolstered her courage, and the little voice again urged her to share her feelings. The truth was, she loved him too much to hide them. Let him see her weak and vulnerable. She had to confess no matter what.

"When do you think the girls will be back?" he asked, oblivious of her daring decision.

"Any time now. Before they get here, I need to tell you something I couldn't say the other night. I'm ready to do that now." Despite a bad case of nerves, she swallowed and plunged ahead. "I want you to know the real reason I ended our relationship."

He gave her such a guarded look. "Who is he?"

"Who is ... What are you talking about?"

"Just tell me."

She could hardly believe her ears. "At times, the words that come out of your mouth astonish me. There's no one else. Only you. I've fallen in love with you again. That's why I ended things the other night. I was scared you'd reject me if you knew, and I couldn't bear that."

She caught her breath and waited for him to do just that, agreeing that in backing away, she'd done the right thing. Instead, he said something entirely different.

"That's funny, and I don't mean the laughing kind. I know exactly how you feel. The other day, while we talked about the girls and when to tell them about us, I realized that I love you. I wasn't going to tell you for

the same reasons, and now here I am, admitting it."
He shook his head and gave a wry smile. "Looks like
we love each other. How did this happen, when neither of us wanted that? What a pair we are. We must
be out of our minds." He took hold of her hands. "The
truth is, I never stopped loving you. My world without
you in it is dull and empty. What I mean is, I don't
know how I can survive without you."

He'd blown her away. Suddenly she had to hold
him. "When you put it like that ..." She let go of his
grasp and started to move into his arms.

"Hold on there," he said, stepping back. "That
apron is wet and I need to take my coat off." He
shrugged out of it and set it aside while she got rid of
the apron, then tugged her in close.

Heaven. "What if we try to be a real couple and fail
like before?" she said, because it could happen.

"We're older and wiser than we were, and when we
have issues we're going to talk them through. No more
keeping things from each other."

"I accept your terms, Mr. Carver. I have a confes-
sion—the second reason I didn't tell you the other
night. I didn't want to seem weak and vulnerable." She
snorted. "Another 'lesson' from my mother."

"Your vulnerability isn't a sign of weakness, it's a
sign of strength and one reason why I love you. You're
the strongest woman I know."

Her heart swelled with love. "Got it. Now kiss me,
will ya?"

"My pleasure." He drew her into a kiss that lasted
until the front door clicked open.

"The girls," Jenny said, and they jerked apart.
"What are we going to do now?"

"Tell them the truth."

27

"So if they won't tell us what's going on, we're calling friends and asking if we can stay at their house," Maddie reminded her sister as they walked up the driveway to their mom's.

"If we can find anyone whose parents will let us," Britt said. "They might not have room."

"Mom and Dad won't know that. Let's go in."

Ready to confront them, Maddie and Britt stomped inside. To Maddie's surprise, their parents were holding hands and smiling.

Thunderstruck, she forgot she was mad at them. "What's up with you two?" she asked as she pulled her coat off.

Britt left hers on and crossed her arms. "Why are you holding hands?"

"We have something to tell you," their mom said and looked at their dad. "Why don't you do the honors."

He wore a huge smile. "Your mother and I are getting back together."

Maddie was speechless, and so was Britt. "But Mom was crying the other day, and you left without saying good night."

"You knew I was crying? I tried to hide that from you." Her mother looked sheepish. "I was too nervous to tell your dad I loved him, so I broke up with him instead."

"Around then, I realized I love her, too," their dad added. "We want to be together as a family."

To Maddie's horror, *she* broke into tears. Britt gaped at her and her parents widened their eyes. "Why are you crying, Maddie?"

"Because I'm happy," she sobbed. "All my life, I wished for this, even when I knew it could never happen. Now it has."

Britt cast them a worried look. "But what if it doesn't last?"

Their parents stared at each other. "I don't blame you for wondering," their mom said. "But I know in my soul it will."

Their dad nodded. "That's a promise we mean to keep."

"Pinky finger swear?" Maddie asked.

Their parents locked pinkies and swore. They looked so happy. "It's pretty great, isn't it?" their dad said, and kissed their mom. Right in front of them.

"Ick," Maddie said, but couldn't stop grinning through the tears.

They pulled apart. "Don't you have to get to your grandparents' now?" Jenny asked.

"You should come with us," Britt said. "Can she, Dad?"

"I don't know. They're not expecting me," their mom said, frowning. "Besides, I couldn't eat another bite."

"Come be with us anyway. My folks will be thrilled. Why don't you call your father, too?"

"I will, and please give your parents a heads-up so they aren't too surprised."

"Wait. Are you going to move in together?" Britt asked.

Their mom nodded. "We haven't gotten that far yet, but it's going to happen."

Maddie and Britt grabbed hands and jumped up and down.

After the calls had been made, the four of them piled into the car. Their other grandpa and Adelle promised to stop by, too.

"This is the best Thanksgiving ever," Maddie said.

Their mom turned in her seat and smiled at them. "I think so, too. I have a hunch there'll be lots more celebrations to come."

Maddie knew in her heart that would happen.

HOURS LATER, as happy as Jenny could remember being in forever, she cuddled on Rob's lap in his living room while they made plans for the future. The girls were asleep. "The twins and the rest of the family seem as happy as we are," she said. "Isn't it wonderful? Wait'll we tell our friends."

"I doubt any of them will be surprised."

"Shawn was right, about us. He pointed out we had feelings for each other and weren't sure what to do about them, so we butted heads instead."

"He's smarter than we were."

"Not anymore." They smiled at each other, and Rob pulled her into a tender kiss. Her heart overflowed with love and joy. "I think you should move in with me—I have more room," she said.

"I'd like that." He stroked his chin. "I hate to sell my place, though. It's a good little house."

"Then hold on to it and rent it out."

"That's a great idea. Rafe owns a lot of rentals and has a ton of experience. I'll ask him for advice."

"I'm sure he'll have lots to give. Speaking of Rafe, when do you want to tell him and the rest of the team?"

"How about tomorrow morning? It's too late tonight, and I'm beat. Plus, I want you in my bed STAT. Ready to turn in?"

"But the girls ... Do you think we should?"

"Definitely. They'll have to get used to us sleeping together, 'cause this time around is for good. For the rest of our lives, I belong to you and you belong to me."

Feeling like she was on top of the world, Jenny rested her forehead against his. "I love you, Rob Carver, and I always will," she promised, then sealed the vow with a long, passionate kiss. "But we have to be really quiet in bed."

"I think we can do that. No time like the present to find out."

Sometime later, sated and wrapped in his arms, Jenny sighed with contentment.

"We did it, Rob—kept quiet."

Having already fallen asleep, he didn't reply.

She laughed softly and knew the next time a problem or concern arose, they'd solve it together. That certainty was her last thought before she drifted off beside him.

The End

ALSO BY ANN ROTH

ABOUT THE AUTHOR

Ann Roth is an award-winning author of 40-plus contemporary romance and women's fiction novels, as well as novellas and numerous short stories. Her first novel was published in 2000 by Harlequin Special Edition and was nominated by *Romantic Times* as best first book. Ann lives with the love of her life in the Greater Seattle area and enjoys creating flawed characters and putting them in challenging situations that help them grow and ultimately find love— whether or not they're looking for it.

Find out about new releases!
Sign up for my newsletter

Or visit my website www.annroth.net